I0638376

READERS *LOVE* BOOKS BY **LINCOLN PARK**;

and here are some of the online comments

they've posted...

"I hope **LINCOLN PARK** *writes another novel. I, for one, will
be first in line to read it!"*
--KATT ROSE

'... **LINCOLN PARK** *-as-narrator has managed to become an
obscure, Hitchcockian character in her own tales! She has
mastered the use of obscenities and figurative context in
relationship to raw storytelling... Frankly, I'm a new fan! "*
-- JULIA JOYCE

"I highly recommend (**LINCOLN PARK** *'S) book to any who
doubt the existence of new, literary talent."* -- DESINRES

"This book was off the hook... can't wait for the next ones... "
-- ARIEL BENJAMIN

" **LINCOLN PARK** *is a gifted writer."*
-- The RAWSISTAZ Reviewers

ALSO BY **LINCOLN PARK**:

Sculptured Nails and NAPPY HAIR

ISBN 1-4116-4062-4

The Brevity of the Selves

ISBN 978-06151-6685-8

HANDLE TIME

LINCOLN

PARK

HANDLE TIME

Copyright © 2008

4465 PreSS

ISBN 978-0-6152-1518-1

All rights reserved. No part of this book may be reproduced in any form, except for the inclusion of brief quotations in a review or article, without express written permission from the author or publisher.

WWW.4465PRESS.COM

HANDLE TIME is a work of fiction. All names, characters and incidents are products of the author's imagination or are used fictitiously. Any resemblance to actual events or persons, living or dead is entirely coincidental. Any references to real people, events, establishments, organizations or locales are intended only to give the fiction a sense of reality and authenticity. Other names, character incidents are either the product of the author's imagination or are used fictitiously; as are those fictionalized events and incidents which may involve real persons and did not occur or are set in the future.

Dedicated
To
all The
Call Center
Workers
in
North america

Overworked and Underpaid Superstars

TABLE OF AUX CODES

HANDLE TIME

"It took a long time for people to realize that the most terrible place one can be banished for all time is not the hell of mythology – the hell Orpheus descended to in order to find his loved Eurydice – nor the hell of the Hebrews or of the Old Testament, nor the hell of Christianity, but the hell of humanity, the hell made by humans for other humans." -- Jacinto Lageira

Call Centers are Hell.

Working in one for *DELSTAR* bank almost *killed* me, literally. The

last thing I remember is how embarrassed I felt while they

were hauling my ass out on a gurney to a waiting ambulance. Never

mind that I could hardly breathe and my heart was racing like a

NASCAR dragster; people were *looking* at me... ruining their daily adherence just to stare at me! I believe a few of them were probably

jealous of me because I was leaving the building and *they* had to get

back on the phones...

At the hospital, the morphine they gave me was *not*

helping. The muscle under my left breast was swept up in a waltz of

spasms and my mother was blowing up my cellphone every five

minutes. The gummy glue, from the stick-on electrodes they'd

plastered me with in the ambulance earlier, was decimating my

décolletage with glops of drying, chafing goo.

Who knew that answering one more call, from one more insatiable,

discourteous, yapaholic customer would land me squat on a stretcher

and in the Emergency Room – just in freaking time for a lukewarm,

lime-*jello* lunch? Trust me – there was no fresh beef to be *had*,

that afternoon; for I was wounded cattle. I had been corralled in the

barn of a bank's regional call center; and I'd spent the past nine months

of my life chewing on the cud of a living wage and grazing on the

grass of shift-diffed pastures. At the end, I'd reduced my stock of

personal pride and professional integrity to a stewed, unsavory, morphine-laced **mutton** – rolling the dough of my ass and the blood in my arteries into a confluence of coagulated *fatty* -- flavored with the remaining teaspoon of my self-esteem and the pungent spice of my jaded spirit.

You know -- not to get off the subject of my E.R. visit – but I know something that you probably don't:

I know why the caged bird drinks.

It's because he once flew (before his caged captivity) onto a sill, and peered through a random, plate-glass window at a *DELSTAR* bank call center.

COACHING

Nobody should have to go into a call center alone, the way I had to. So -- I thought I'd use this section of the book to give you some idea of what the call center experience is like (Don't worry. We'll get to my story in due course).

PRE-SHIFT AUX

As soon as a Customer Service Rep, Tech Support Rep, Digital Banker – or any other kind of telephone contact agent -- gets inside of a call center building at the beginning of their assigned shift, they put themselves in **pre-shift aux** and *head for the break rooms.* You didn't know? Call center break rooms are the **STUFF OF LEGEND**.

On a typical day; after surviving the morning's crushed ice attack, employees scramble to this special room for coffee as if their very lives depended on it! Heaven could but help the first customer of the worker who couldn't get a sugar-substitute packet for their java jolt.

In this hallowed room, vending machines spit out things like:

- bent cups which are filled with dirty water (*posing as Premium Blend*) ,
- pre-squished oatmeal cookies in cheery and child-proofed, plastic wrappers ,
- lukewarm bottles of soda with the (*expired*) sweepstakes' '*PLEASE TRY AGAIN*' *twist-caps*...

... all while sucking up bills and change like those pricey, candy-colored

vacuum cleaners they have out now with the super-duper, suction action!

The refrigerators in the break rooms are replete with moldy *Tupperware*; while white, superstore-plastic, grocery bags full of expired microwave meals lie on top of each other in a frozen, odoriferous

orgy. Speaking of microwaves, these boxy, nuclear weapons are a matter of sectional hierarchy in the call center environment. Low-level operatives who want to nuke their snacks get a rancid, rusty, white metal box with a dial to use. However, if you are higher up on the employment food-chain, *your* break room would have a charcoal-gray, or black microwave with modern, specialized buttons – like a popcorn key.

ARCHETYPES

No matter what call center you may work in, call up or visit, you will run across some of the same type of people. Why? Because the Human Resources departments at call centers can smell the desperation on the applicants as soon as they walk through the door. Only the truly needy, broke and spastic apoplectic gets hired. Below, I've listed the personality types of some of the call center regulars I've come to know and love:

- **POLITICOS** - After they've known you for about two weeks, they sit a table away from you in the cafeteria and try their best to goad you into a political discussion – so they can trash the party they oppose (*which is probably the one you favor*).

- **"Red Dye" Mafia** – There's always some bitch with a bad cellophane or otherwise, botched red-dye job. *Always.*

- **Know It Alls** - The Power of Christ compels them to correct someone... even if that someone is in complete agreement with them.

- **Soldiers of Fortune** - The nerd who goes postal. The floozy with the Uzi. The techie with a Tech-9. The grunger with the Glock. Hopefully, security has already escorted them off the premises and handed them over to the cops by the time you learn that you just swapped days off with one of them.

- **aCTION HEROES** -- ...all over the desks, the t-shirts, the lunchboxes, the cellphone faceplates, etc.... I don't get it. I mean - Bruce Wayne, Professor Xavier and Tony Stark were all rich! Okay - so Peter Parker was poor; but even *he* had sense enough not to work in a call center! What a waste of webbing that would have been! LOL

- **GamERS** -- Their entire life revolves around the purchase of the next version of the **same, inane videogame (S.I.V.)**. They keep fooling themselves that one day they will win big, prize money in a national gaming competition.... if only they could get **S.I.V. – VERSION 8.5** within the first 45 minutes of when it gets released next year!

- **VaNILLa ICeS** - After every thing they say comes a one, or two verse impromptu rhyme. Whadd'ya know it – your co-worker's a poet.

- **PHILOSOPHERS** - Everything they say is supposed to be from some sort of deep, existential standpoint; but the sad truth is that they are legends in their own minds.

- ## THE neUROTICaLLY DOWnTRODDen
  - These people are perpetually and pathetically depressed; and somehow, being rewarded with a bi-weekly paycheck for services rendered is even a cause for sadness.

- ## anGLeRS - Beware. These slimy fuckers would sell you out for a dress-down patch.

- ## DeGReeDniKS - These people will never miss a chance to tell you about the advanced, university degrees they hold; or how much money they used to make. They simply cannot accept the fact that in spite of all the post-secondary posturing, they make the same, low-grade pittance as everyone else on the call center floor.

- **OPPOSITIZENS** (*my personal favorites*) - Whatever you may say to these people, they are **going** to say the **opposite**. Every single and solitary response they *give* you starts with,

"Well, no, not really.

Actually..." Don't fight with these people. You will **never** be correct. All you will ever be is amazed at the stupidity and the effort these people expend to prove that you do not have the right idea, answer or inkling about anything the two of you ever discuss. When you see them coming, just say 'hi' and keep walking.

OH, THE HR-OR

In a call center, *everything* you do – outside of taking customer calls – is a potential

HR (*Human Resources*) issue.

If you ask a question, you are insubordinate. If you try to blink a fleck of dust from your eye and someone from the opposite sex sees you, they have been sexually harassed. If you're the sort who eats in the cafeteria and takes the time to chew your food, you will eventually, be 'coached' about your poor schedule adherence. Why? Because digesting

your meals is an HR issue:

"THE SCHEDULING DEPARTMENT SAYS THAT YOU'RE TAKING TOO LONG TO EAT. WE ARE NOT SUGGESTING THAT YOU GAG WHILE YOU ARE EATING, BUT PERHAPS YOU CAN EAT JUST A LITTLE MORE DILIGENTLY? WE HAVE AN HR TRAINING CLASS COMING UP ABOUT THAT. IT'S CALLED, *"TARGETED CONSUMPTION"*. IF YOU SIGN UP FOR THE CLASS, YOU CAN PUT YOURSELF IN COACHING AUX WHILE YOU ARE IN THE CLASSROOM."

If you cuss in a bathroom stall because your period started and you forgot to bring pads to work – you'd better hope you weren't overheard by some 'holier-than-thou' sort of colleague. Profanity is an HR issue, damnit!

"A COMPLAINT WAS FILED BY SOMEONE IN A BATHROOM STALL NEXT TO YOU. THEY WERE OFFENDED BY YOUR USE OF PROFANITY. ONCE THE COMPLAINT WAS FILED, WE **HAD** TO WRITE IT UP. WE'D LIKE YOU TO SIGN THIS COMPLAINT ON THE BOTTOM OF THE PAGE – AS PROOF THAT YOU HAVE READ THE CONTENTS OF THE COMPLAINT IN ITS ENTIRETY. OKAY?"

If your father is on his death-bed, see to it that he remains in this world until your paid vacation time is approved. Unscheduled days off are an HR issue:

"WE DO UNDERSTAND THAT BOTH OF YOUR PARENTS DIED IN THE CAR ACCIDENT WE SAW ON THE NEWS LAST WEEK... SORRY FOR YOUR LOSS. BUT FROM THE COMPANY'S STANDPOINT – WE NEED PEOPLE IN THE CHAIRS WHEN THEY ARE SCHEDULED TO BE THERE. WE SIMPLY **CANNOT** GIVE YOU THAT MUCH TIME TO SHIP THEIR BODIES TO THEIR CHILDHOOD HOME FOR A FUNERAL. CAN YOU POSSIBLY

HAVE THE FUNERAL LOCALLY? WOULD YOU LIKE THE NAME OF A REPUTABLE CREMATORY?"

What's in a name

It boggles the mind to figure out why the following is necessary, but HR departments in call centers like to call themselves all *kinds* of vacuous and vainglorious voop. I mean, they will call themselves

anything from **Firemen to Landscape Architects**; but never *Human* *Resources* or *Personnel*. Depending on the center, they can be masked as *People Movers, Team Experience Specialists, Workforce Development Engineers, Resource Procurement Generalists, Dynamic Capital Technicians, Workflow Deployment Managers* or *Site Cohabitation Units.*

even MORE HR-OR

Another, enigmatic thing that comes from the anal and arrested mind of someone in one of these cattle-rustling, people-firing departments -- is one of the greatest anomalies of our contemporary age. I'm referring to

the ostensible offerings of **pizza** and **chili** -- *two of the most gastric, intestinally non-compliant foodstuffs on the*

face of the Earth --

– as performance incentives to clusters of cubicled captives; who regurgitate the recirculated air of call centers. Attempting to fathom the fierceness of the funk from all the farting, the base and belligerent belching and the afterglow of the occasional upchuck is impossible...

... even with the power of the most expensive and descriptive pen.

IT'S POTTY TIME

Call center bathrooms and the stalls therein are fluorescent

sanctuary. These are the heroes; the lacquered-metal

stations that share a curious cacophony (*of sounds, smells, gossip, grand ideas and piped-in pop hits*) with faux-stone sinks and spigots of stainless steel (*that spew hard water on everything but the hands they were intended to wash*).

Excursions of the temporarily excused are often flights of payday fantasy; with checks being spent on cars, furs, jewels, videogaming, Internet porn, backyard playground equipment and magnanimous

investments – all between grunts – glorious to some, grueling to others.

17

This is also where workers can exact sweet revenge on the HR staff. Trapped and occupied in a solitary stall, the HR representative must endure diatribes of swearing and linguistic lacerations of the management team by neighboring stalls of crapping co-workers.

If you've ever washed your hands in a call center sink, though, you know that as your hands get wet and you dread returning to your seat on the floor, the water from the faucet doesn't feel like water, at all. Rather, it feels like you are slathering your hands with a lukewarm, slimebath...

...the same lukewarm slimebath your life has become. You are a **low-level employee from sector 7G**, and that's it.

Sector 7G

LUNGS ON

LINE 3...

You cannot **believe** how much of a call center worker's salary goes to cigarettes! Fully, 95% of the employees smoke.

India is partially to blame; but you can also make the case that sucking and blowing hot air is an expression of disdain and helplessness.

Actually, the smoking is a by-product of the *real* activity; which is the

preparation to smoke. Agents run out to caress their cancer canes like the faithful who herd into arenas to see the Pope. I know this for a fact, because I have been witness to both events.

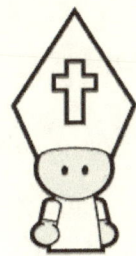

Once a smoker has identified another smoker on the floor, a clandestine relationship ensues. IMs and emails to consolidate break schedules fly back-and-forth; photographs of secondhand smoke-suffering offspring are shown off; and unspoken canons of contempt for non-smoking co-workers is carefully passed from veteran puffer to novice; under protection of watchful eyes and hushed tones.

On the other hand, the non-smokers in call centers can be compared to the Bene Gesserit in the movie, *Dune*. There was always one (*smoke-filled*) place, deep in the call center, where the non-smokers dare not venture – lest all manner of illness befall them. LOLOLOL!

SECURITY

OH *YEAH*, BABY, YOUR ass IS BEING *WATCHED*

in a call center. The cameras have the most

phallic shape, too. I used to call security, 'DICKWATCH' because of that. Also, because the people watching you on the other end were usually mindless, nondescript dicks.

Neither *Nostradamus, George Orwell, Ray Bradbury,* nor any other

paranoid, schizoid, or futuristic

fatalist could have imagined the degree of monitoring and tracking that goes on per person, in a call center! Cute, little demi-bubbles of smoky-colored plastic inhabit every eleventh square of drop-ceiling. The bubbles provide cover for cameras that can unzip any blouse and zoom onto any bosom-heaving beauty mark on the floor..

...Keystrokes and screenshots of innocent, hardworking computer desktops are captured for the sole purpose of career 'coaching' and other criticisms directed toward the agent – otherwise known as

CORRECTIVE ACTION.

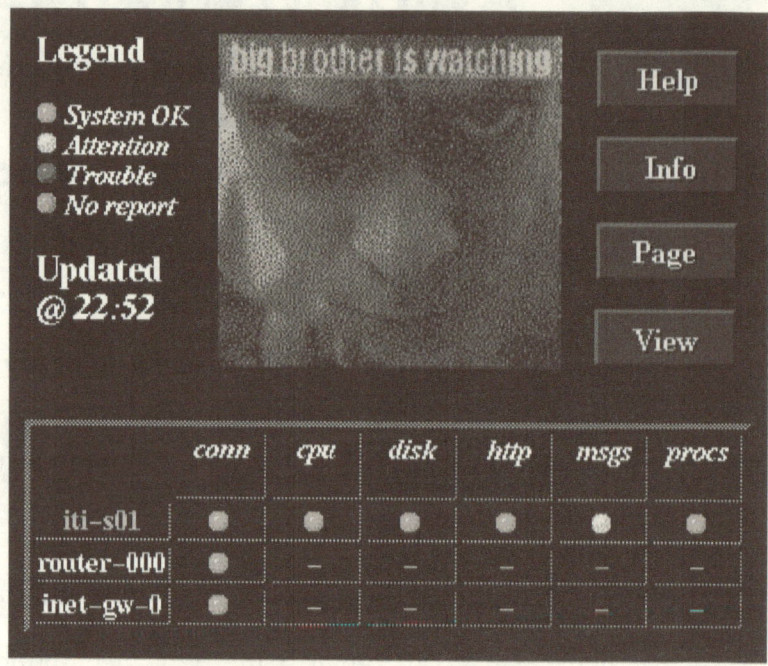

ACTIVE ALLEY

Every call center has *some* kind of retarded, 'Rumpus Room'; complete with a pool table, air hockey and two or three TVs. Also -- and most importantly -- this room would have a set of stupid, house rules; and a nonsensical name like **HAPPY HALL, FUN COUNTRY, REC-WORLD, PIT-STOP, THE BREAK MACHINE**... whatever. The 'Rumpus Room' at *DELSTAR* bank was called **ACTIVE ALLEY**.

In *Active Alley*, you could do anything you wanted to, except *rumpus, be active, be happy, take a break* or *have fun*. Here is a breakdown of the basic rules:

- **NO FOOD** – Okay, so that means, your lunchtime is screwed. Not just because you can't eat there -- but because *Active Alley* is just that; an active room in an alley WAY, WAY on the farthest side of the call center; at least twenty minutes walking distance from any other place an employee would frequent... like the

cafeteria, for example.

- **EMPLOYEES ONLY** – Considering that you practically have to have a retina scan outside every morning before the call center doors will open for you; this rule may seem a tad bit obvious. Just a tad.

- **DO NOT REARRANGE FURNITURE** – Yeah. Like you are just *dying* to give up your lunch break to practice interior decorating with buttcrack-scented settees (which have all been screwed into the floor, BTW).

- **PICK UP TRASH AND THROW IT AWAY** - *What* trash? You can't have *food* in Active Alley!

- **PUT POOL CUES, CHALK, PING-PONG BALLS, ETC. UP** – You could, if the call center had supplied them in the first place... *I* said they had a pool *table* in *Active Alley*. I didn't say anything about them having balls, cues or chalk!

- **LEAVE CUSHIONS ON CHAIRS (THEY ARE NOT PILLOWS)** – This, I'm afraid, is a tall order. Most who brave the time-consuming excursion to *Active Alley* are there for some serious,

shut-eye; some hard-core, uncensored *inactivity* -- before returning to three or four more hours of rabid customers; cussing and foaming their frothy, foul-mouthed tirades through the telephone lines. You'd better damn well *believe* that the chair cushions in *Active Alley* are subject to *actively* hold the heavy heads of *DELSTAR* bank's distraught and fatigued phone reps, at any given time.

SEX IN THE AUX

FRIDAY
IS CASUAL
SEX DAY

Call center sex is wanton, unprotected and reckless – especially in

India – but back to the point: The unused meeting rooms in the

DELSTAR call center were business-hour bastions of the most scurvy,

grungy adultery. One of the 'soops' (*supervisors*) on our floor had his ass

hauled off by security for whipping his dick out in the *Freesia* conference

room.... and that brings up another point:

What the fuck is the deal with the names of these conference rooms? In call centers, they can be names of cars, exotic animals, names of cities dotting Interstate-70, flowers... it's ridiculous! Whatever happened to good ol',

Conference Room A?

Anyway, there are thousands of call-center-made babies roaming the Earth at any given time; as evidenced by the existence of the zillions of

push-pin damaged, toddler photos speckling the cubicle message boards throughout the building. The main concern of a call center though, is that these infants are conceived within the boundaries of a worker's scheduled breaks. For you see -- society may have room for the waif born out of wedlock these days, but only *Heaven* can help the

baby who is born out of adherence!

DEFCON AUX

First there was the piercing pitch of the digital sirens. Then, emergency lights flashed on and off. As the customer in your ear screamed for your undivided attention and explanation as to why a six-pack of beer had put his bank account into a double digit overdraft – a random manager would come by and scream for you to go into *Aux999*. We were definitely in DEFCON AUX:

"People - LOGOFF YOUR PHONES RIGHT NOW. LET'S GO!"

People would barrel down the stairs -- trying not to think about those who got stuck in the satanic stairwells of *September 11th*. On the way out of the building, there were always a few idiots who went to their cars and sat inside. Thank God there was never an actual explosion in, or around the facility. From what I can recall, the scariest thing that happened at *DELSTAR* during the time I was there, was that

somebody started a fire in a trash can. They made 1500

people logout of their stations -- and lose their

monthly commissions – just because some

GENIUS set fire to his employment application and put it in a metal fucking trash can!

nUKe-TRITION

Call center cafeterias have a grand design: to reclaim any disposable income the workers may have after living expenses, from paycheck-to-paycheck.

In *DELSTAR*, the cafeteria was in the basement of the building. Note that I said in the *basement* – yet

every day, like Clockwork

Smurf -- People scrambled to

the farthest corners and reaches

of the lunchroom - trying to find

cellphone reception. It was the
craziest thing I'd ever seen!

In *DELSTAR*'s cafeteria, I would usually use my lunch time to rock out with my portable CD player. I know it would have sounded better in the book if I'd said an *iPod*, but I just couldn't justify shelling out 400 dollars for one when burning CDs was so easy and economical. I mean, *Big Stocks* in the mall near my house sells a stack of 100, recordable CDs for three dollars and change. Besides – have you seen my *light* bill? *DELSTAR* barely paid me enough to keep my *cellphone* on a charger!

The girls who worked in the cafeteria were relatively tight knit; as they all had the same outsourced employer, *POSTAMARK*.

Most of the other girls I worked with never socialized with the cafeteria 'help', but you could hear *me* laughing and carrying on with them at least once or twice a day!

I loved them.

The older ladies in the call center cafeteria sat alongside each other and talked about their backyard gardening – or the new drapes they just bought, or something. The younger girls praddled on about their 'man'; or the calorie count of the lunch they were eating, and so on.

The guys in the lunchroom would usually lead off their conversations with nonchalant references to T.O.'s latest press conference. If you were a regular at the table, they might throw in a crack about a couple of passing 'racks':

"Day-um," seemed to be the most prevalent crack.

Okay – so the cafeteria at *DELSTAR* wasn't that bad. I can't complain; at least we *had* one. I know that some call centers have to hope some vendor shows up two days-a-week; to serve hellishly hot meals at hellishly high prices. Still, if you wanted to take home any salary at all from *DELSTAR*, you would have to get used to nuking your food.

" I wish I'd invented microwave meals!"
"You and me, both!"

Nuked food sucks, but it's so easy and convenient to throw six or seven boxes of food into your shopping cart; especially if you can get a box for under three dollars! The cubed, MDF (*medium-density fiberboard*) they try to pass off in these meals as chicken, beef or turkey chunks, even seems to be **tasting** more like chicken, beef or turkey chunks, these days! Still takes you 45 minutes to **chew it**, however.

I used 4(min):30(sec) as my 'nuking' default. Any less time, the food would still have ice chips on it when I took it out of the microwave. Any *more* time, my lunch period would basically, be over.

It's funny – but when you eat lunch near a microwave oven, you pay attention to the stupidest things... like who's standing at the cash register... the dried gum on the floor next to your right foot... why the sea is boiling hot... whether pigs have wings...

Have a Happy...

Holiday time at a call center is a unique experience. They go completely *berserk,* if you ask *me.*

For the one *Thanksgiving* that I was employed there, *DELSTAR* gave

out **free turkeys** from the back of a minivan, parked outside the service entrance.

I decided to give the turkey I received to a young Latina who was working in the building as a custodian. The girls in the lunchroom told me that she had to choose between giving her kids Christmas – or Thanksgiving dinner; because she didn't have the coin to do both.

"*That's so sweet. Who does that?*" The girls in the cafeteria crowded around me and offered me a free lunch for being so nice.

"Are you kidding? I live alone," I said; "I'm not cooking *that*... I'd be eating turkey for the next fifteen months! Turkey sandwiches, turkey soup, turkey salad, turkey burgers, turkey casserole, turkey pizza..."

"Enough, Chase. We *get* it,." Everybody laughed; and I handed over my turkey to one of the cooks in the cafeteria kitchen.

I wanted the whole thing to be anonymous – so after I left the turkey in the lunchroom, I just went about my business – and got back on the phones. When the young lady tried to leave the building with the turkey, she got cut off at the pass by the brawny butch from Environmental Services; who yanked her by the ear – and pulled her straight into the security office.

It took me a half-hour, off the phones and out-of-adherence, to convince security that I was *giving* her my turkey; and that she wasn't stealing it from the cafeteria freezers. *So much for anonymity.* Happy freaking holidays.

METRICS

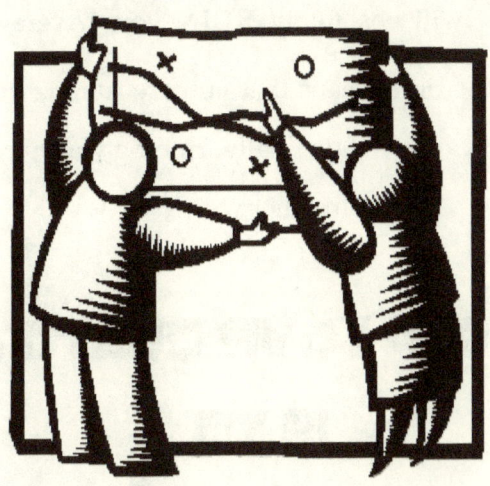

While the customer thinks they are the most important aspect of a

call center's life; it is the metrics which actually reigns supreme.

The measurement of *Quality* of service to customers only serves as a

way to block payout of commission-based incentives. Centers rely on

Sales, Average Handle Time (AHT),

Quality and Schedule Adherence to justify

everything from the purchase of toilet paper to their reason for continued

existence.

In call centers, to take time and help your customer will absolutely RUIN your Average Handle Time. Ruining your handle time means that you are ruining your quality; thus, ruining your agent variable pay; finally, ruining your paycheck.

In other words:

TO HELP YOUR CUSTOMER IS TO COMPLETELY AND UNEQUIVOCALLY, RUIN YOUR PAYCHECK.

I'm *serious*! The idea is to stay on the call for the shortest amount of time that you can; in order for you to take as many calls as you can. The customer's satisfaction with your service is incidental. And so – every call center worker must ponder the following questions and make a choice each time they logon to their systems:

DO I

HELP THE CUSTOMER?

– OR –

DO I PAY RENT?

SS NR-GA 0670200

DEPARTMENT OF HOUSING

EVICTION NOTICE

Please be advised that your home will be ransacked, doused in gasoline and torched to the ground as of 9pm tonight.

DPS-39 (10-93)

CHUMP CHANGE

Call centers pay their workers through the combination of an

ancient Chinese secret called *Agent Base Pay* and

some adjunct form of rocket science called *Agent Variable Pay.*

$$\ddot{x} = \frac{1}{M-ml}\left\{mc_e + F_n(p - p_{atm}\,e^{-(k/H)(\sqrt{(x^2+y^2+z^2)}-H)})\right\}\cos\alpha(t) - g_0R^2\frac{x}{(x^2+y^2+z^2)^{3/2}} +$$
$$- \frac{c_w(\sqrt{(\dot{x}^2+\dot{y}^2+\dot{z}^2)},\chi)}{M-ml}\rho_0\,e^{-(1/H)(\sqrt{(x^2+y^2+z^2)}-H)}\,F\dot{x}\sqrt{(\dot{x}^2+\dot{y}^2+\dot{z})} +$$
$$+ \frac{c_a(\sqrt{(\dot{x}^2+\dot{y}^2+\dot{z}^2)},\chi)}{M-ml}\rho_0\,e^{-(1/H)(\sqrt{(x^2+y^2+z^2)}-H)}\,F\times$$
$$\times\frac{\dot{z}\{\dot{z}\cos\alpha(t)-\dot{x}\cos\gamma(t)\}-\dot{y}\{\dot{x}\cos\beta(t)-\dot{y}\cos\alpha(t)\}\sqrt{(\dot{x}^2+\dot{y}^2+\dot{z}^2)}}{\sqrt{[\{\dot{y}\cos\gamma(t)-\dot{z}\cos\beta(t)\}^2+\{\dot{z}\cos\alpha(t)-\dot{x}\cos\gamma(t)\}^2+\{\dot{x}\cos\beta(t)-\dot{y}\cos\alpha(t)\}^2]}} + 2\dot{y}\omega + \omega^2 x$$

$$\ddot{y} = \frac{1}{M-ml}\left\{mc_e + F_n(p - p_{atm}\,e^{-(k/H)(\sqrt{(x^2+y^2+z^2)}-H)})\right\}\cos\beta(t) - g_0R^2\frac{y}{(x^2+y^2+z^2)^{3/2}} +$$
$$- \frac{c_w(\sqrt{(\dot{x}^2+\dot{y}^2+\dot{z}^2)},\chi)}{M-ml}\rho_0\,e^{-(1/H)(\sqrt{(x^2+y^2+z^2)}-H)}\,F\dot{y}\sqrt{(\dot{x}^2+\dot{y}^2+\dot{z}^2)} +$$
$$+ \frac{c_a(\sqrt{(\dot{x}^2+\dot{y}^2+\dot{z}^2)},\chi)}{M-ml}\rho_0\,e^{-(1/H)(\sqrt{(x^2+y^2+z^2)}-H)}\,F\times$$
$$\times\frac{\dot{x}\{\dot{x}\cos\beta(t)-\dot{y}\cos\alpha(t)\}-\dot{z}\{\dot{y}\cos\gamma(t)-\dot{z}\cos\beta(t)\}\sqrt{(\dot{x}^2+\dot{y}^2+\dot{z})}}{\sqrt{[\{\dot{y}\cos\gamma(t)-\dot{z}\cos\beta(t)\}^2+\{\dot{z}\cos\alpha(t)-\dot{x}\cos\gamma(t)\}^2+\{\dot{x}\cos\beta(t)-\dot{y}\cos\alpha(t)\}^2]}} - 2\dot{x}\omega + \omega^2 y$$

$$\ddot{z} = \frac{1}{M-ml}\left\{mc_e + F_n(p - p_{atm}\,e^{-(k/H)(\sqrt{(x^2+y^2+z^2)}-H)})\right\}\cos\gamma(t) - g_0R^2\frac{z}{(x^2+y^2+z^2)^{3/2}} +$$
$$- \frac{c_w(\sqrt{(\dot{x}^2+\dot{y}^2+\dot{z}^2)},\chi)}{M-ml}\rho_0\,e^{-(1/H)(\sqrt{(x^2+y^2+z^2)}-H)}\,F\dot{z}\sqrt{(\dot{x}^2+\dot{y}^2+\dot{z}^2)} + \frac{c_a(\sqrt{(\dot{x}^2+\dot{y}^2+\dot{z}^2)},\chi)}{M-ml}\rho_0\times$$
$$\times\,e^{-(1/H)(\sqrt{(x^2+y^2+z^2)}-H)}\,F\frac{\dot{y}\{\dot{y}\cos\gamma(t)-\dot{z}\cos\beta(t)\}-\dot{x}\{\dot{z}\cos\alpha(t)-\dot{x}\cos\gamma(t)\}\sqrt{(\dot{x}^2+\dot{y}^2+\dot{z})}}{\sqrt{[\{\dot{y}\cos\gamma(t)-\dot{z}\cos\beta(t)\}^2+\{\dot{z}\cos\alpha(t)-\dot{x}\cos\gamma(t)\}^2+\{\dot{x}\cos\beta(t)-\dot{y}\cos\alpha(t)\}^2]}}$$

in which: $\chi = \arccos\dfrac{\dot{x}\cos\alpha(t)+\dot{y}\cos\beta(t)+\dot{z}\cos\gamma(t)}{\sqrt{(\dot{x}^2+\dot{y}^2+\dot{z}^2)}}$

In effect, to understand the way you get paid in a call center is to be more than qualified to work in the call center most Americans refer to as,

MISSION CONTROL.

Basically, you should just be happy you get a paycheck, at all. If the

check you get at your call center is **anything** like my checks were at *DELSTAR*, the IRS takes a third; healthcare, social-security and your landlord take half of what's left; and maybe you'll get enough to put a quarter-tank of gas in your car...

... but that's only **after** the call center penalizes your check and takes

your **commission bonus** away, for being just

$2 short on your sales goals for the month.

DUUUDE...

... **Fuck** that shit. What **I** was finally able to understand about

AVP, is that the whole concept of bonus pay in a call center is

imaginary...

... Just like the *rest* of a call center paycheck!

CA$H WARS

Another cultural pigeon-hole of call center life is the socioeconomic divide between those who get paid by **paper check** -vs.- those who have opted to be paid by **EFT**; electronic funds transfer –

otherwise known as, direct deposit. You should know that *DELSTAR* Bank encourages direct deposit; because it saves them money. How do they do this? Easily.

"THOSE OF YOU WHO GET PAID BY PAPER CHECK – KNOW THAT THE EXPRESS MAIL PACKAGES FROM HEADQUARTERS DIDN'T GO OUT UNTIL TODAY – SO – THAT MEANS YOU WON'T HAVE YOUR CHECKS UNTIL TOMORROW; OR WEDNESDAY, AT THE LATEST."

"What about the people who get direct deposit?"

"YOU GUYS' CHECKS SHOULD HAVE POSTED TO YOUR ACCOUNT LAST NIGHT."

They also encourage direct deposit into a *DELSTAR* employee bank account (*Never mind that the only DELSTAR branch in the State of Missouri is a solitary ATM machine on the top floor of the building*).

The Wrath of Khan

People who work in American call centers *hate* India. Not the Indian people, per se; rather the actual, geographical continent. They are completely convinced that the birthplace of the pacifist, *Gandhi*, will also be the birthplace of the prophesied, *Apocalypse*.

At least twice a year, a call center manager is required to threaten his, or her team with news that their center is closing and that their customer queue will be handed over to another headset hegemony of Bollywood phone actors.

Employee newsletters in American call centers frequently show Indian call center workers utilizing flat-screen PC monitors, bluetooth-enabled headsets, wireless keyboards and wireless mice; while smiling ear-to-ear and singing quoted, suck-puppy phrases to the bank for helping them climb the ladder of their country's crappy, caste system. Here's one:

"IF I CANNOT WORK AROUND A PROBLEM, I PULL IN THE REST OF THE TEAM. SOMEONE ALWAYS ARRIVES UPON A SOLUTION AND IT ALWAYS PROVES EFFECTIVE."
                                        -- PARAMESWAR RANGARAJAN

Here's another one:

"SOME OF US WORK OVERTIME WHEN NECESSARY TO TAKE MORE CALLS. THIS INITIATIVE IS ALWAYS ACKNOWLEDGED AND REWARDED EVERY PAY PERIOD."
                                        -- PRAKASH PALATHINGAL

This corporate-sanctioned, derogatory depiction of Indian call center workers is designed to make an American worker feel *so* low – that they could almost imagine a possible benefit to growing up, starving, on the shores of the gangrened Ganges.

FYI -- Site-selection for fast food burger restaurants is based, in direct proportion to the disdain for India-per-call-center-cubic-foot. Why? Because -- for every pang of fear an American call center worker feels over the possibility of their job getting shipped out to India; there exists a hunger pang for a

quartercheese... a juicy, cheesy, charbroiled, *cow* cut - drenched in oozy, ruby red ketchup... the kind of juicy cow cut that just can't cut it in Calcutta.

From a personal standpoint, I never understood why there was such a **disconnect** between ourselves and our Indian colleagues until three of them were flown from the Jaipur call center to Banfield; to give us some specialized training with our customer management system, UNIKRASH.

"Have you heard?"

"No. What."

"The *Indians* are here!"

"So? And we're supposed to - what."

Apparently, two ladies and one man were sent over to train us on the correct process and use of UNIKRASH; which had recently been integrated with our bank fee refund assessment tools. It struck me as odd that they would show up to teach us how to use UNIKRASH - only *after* we had been using it on the floor for at *least* two months.

My initial experience with the ladies occurred in the break room. Right off the bat, I was uncomfortable. Why? Frankly, it was because of the way these women *smelled*. I don't know if was due to the fragrances in their fabrics which were foreign to my nose; or the curry/cumin-laced concoction they were fussing over in a nearby crock-pot; or some ghastly combination of the fabric funk and the food, or *what*. I just know that they didn't smell *fresh* (That's the politest way I can put it. I'm **sorry**. My mother raised me with the elementary concept that women are supposed to smell respectably **fresh** in civilized society). I went straight to the bathroom, so I

could put some industrial soap foam on the tip of my nose and breathe it in (*The bathrooms used to have gel soap; but I'm glad they changed over to the soap foam – it's much cleaner*).

That's not all! When we were assembled in the training room with them at last, one of the ladies referred to our class as a *batch*.

A *batch!*

...Like a batch of cookies; or a

controlled-batch of **bird-**

flu anecdote from the CDC, or some other inanimate object:

"THIS IS A *GOOD* BATCH," she said; "THIS BATCH UNDERSTANDS WHAT WE WERE TRYING TO CONVEY ON THE FIRST ATTEMPT."

Rarely, if ever, had I heard a comment imply such offense; uttered from the mouth of someone who smelled so bad.

NOTE REGARDING ANGRY, SEEMINGLY BIGOTED ENTRIES:

Some people implored me not to put this section in the book - because Indian Call Center workers have, indeed, been subject to **disgusting abuse** from American customers who call them up and carry on. True, but this is *my* story and I defend my entry for several reasons:

- **FIRSTLY**, we get the same, obnoxious, incendiary, American customers in our American call centers. Who do you think the Indian workers transfer those customers *to* when they have had enough? By the way - Indian customers can be just as obnoxious. **NOONE HOLDS A MONOPOLY ON RUDENESS. RUDENESS IS A SHARED AND WORLDWIDE ENTITY, OF CALLERS AND YES, EVEN REPRESENTATIVES, ALIKE. EVERYBODY JUST NEEDS TO STOP BEING SO FUCKING RUDE!**

- **SECONDLY**, there is a best-selling book out by an Indian author that trashes Americans on several occasions. Why can't we express our distaste at their contempt for our easy-to-pronounce names; or their proud declaration of their

35=10 axiom,

which implies that: *The mind of a 35 year old American Adult is equivalent to the mind of a 10 year old Indian child.*

- **THIRDLY**, *those bitches HAD NO SENSE OF* **personal hygiene** *and they called* my class a **batch** — *with a coldness and calculation to rival their celebrated technical*

 *skills and expertise. To this day, that just sticks in my fucking* **craw**.

49

PAGESPACE

Just about everyone who works in an American call center has their own page on **PAGESPACE, YOURSPACE, INSPACE, FACESPACE,** -- whatever -- some kind of social networking space on the World Wide Web. In fact, some dweebs go so far as to create a page for their call center – in the hopes that everybody will become a friend on the call center page. That's a stupid idea – because social networking sites are largely blocked from access to call center workers while they are on the job.

These pages also provide the call-center rep with a sinister sort of booby prize. Their personal spaces at the online social network are their

permanent tickets to a lower-middle-class existence. Front line agents

who have aspirations of ascension to the ranks of

the comfortably banked, are not yet aware of the

malevolent (*and frankly,* odd), web-searching done by prospective

employers for the *tiniest fraction* of free, unobstructed, socially networked

thought. Personnel departments live to the dust the lascivious

lustitude and political bloggypunditry which

may be lurking beneath the quirky email addresses and sassy screen

names belonging to their cordially evasive job applicants.

As a result, **no person, in any company,** who assists customers over a

queued VoIP for more than three months, could *ever* hope to work for

any civic, substantial, professional or political office of any kind. They

could never survive the vetting.

TRINKETOYS

In other professions, companies are tripping over themselves to push every conceivable piece of corporate-branded merchandise down the throats of their employees as they possibly can. From the chartreuse car with the corporate logo splashed on the doors; to the polo shirts with the embroidered logos; to the stuff like calculators and mousepads. They hand out keychains, badge-holders and briefcases; mugs, magnets, squishy balls and pens. **The objective of the enterprise is plain**. It is, to:

1. _**promote the company name**_ _everywhere the employee goes; and have the employee serve as an unpaid, unwitting and perpetual, banner advertisement_
2. _**reinforce the employee's sense of company loyalty**_ _by packing his bag with tons of 'free stuff'; that gets deducted from his salary_

3. **_boost the employee's morale_** *so that he doesn't mind working for*

    peanuts in a thankless job with no chance for advancement

... I mean, if *I* were a retention manager somewhere, that would be *my*

reason for wasting the company's money

on all that superfluous shrubbish ...

... not *DELSTAR*, though. No-sir-*ree*. They actually wanted you to *earn*

their branded coffee cups and pencils! Needless to say, in spite of all the

premium incentives and neat 'freebies' the corporation told their

stockholders were being circulated throughout the rank-and-file; **nobody**

had any kind of *DELSTAR* logo merchandise on their desks.

Paradoxically, while nobody was ever able to earn enough points or

cross enough quality hurdles in their metrics for a flimsy, *DELSTAR*

mousepad or cheap, desk calendar, we *were* able to win some

decent sales-performance gifts, from time to time. Somebody won an

mp3 player once; and even *I* managed to win a couple of

things on the floor. I won a VCR (*never mind that we all use DVDs, now*); a

coffee grinder; a fleece, *DELSTAR-logo* blanket and a *DELSTAR-logo*

backpack. They say that not too long after I left, one of the girls in my

original training class, *Jillian*, won a GameStation 4 and sold it to another colleague of ours, *Joseph*. I don't believe that, though...

she was too self-absorbed to sell her stuff to anyone at work. If they'd told

me that she sold it on *bidBaY*... that, I would believe! LOL

THE DIRECTOR

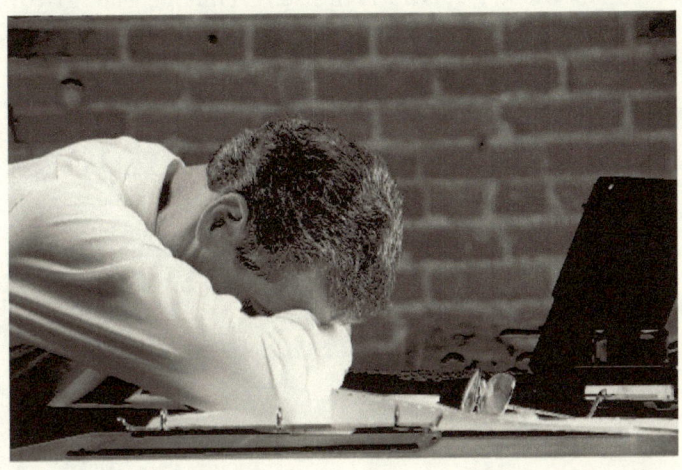

Seeing THE DIRECTOR in a call center is just like trying to find

Elvis. Good *luck*, Buddy.

When I was at DELSTAR, I use to have this fantasy of spotting our director and shooting him with a sleeper dart; so that I could prove to the world that he actually existed. Then, I would drag him to the state's regional lotto office or mining reclamation division and collect my bounty. How much do you think I could get for a call center director? Not much, right? That's why I didn't actually go through with it.

The guys who run call centers are formally known as **Service Delivery Directors.** Armed with pagers, PDAs, pocket protectors and primary-colored polo shirts; these guardians of the *revenue-per-call* gridiron may be spotted at any time; zipping around corners or grabbing their waists as

their portable, electronic devices simultaneously vibrate.

(Sounds just a little  , doesn't

it? LOL)

The primary mission of the Service Delivery Director at our call center was, to keep justifying to *DELSTAR* headquarters why our Banfield, MO call center should stay open. As such, the Director got a weekly,

speakerphone spanking from the bank:

"YOUR PEOPLE IN BANFIELD NEED TO THINK IN TERMS OF KEEPING OUR COST-PER-CALL MINIMIZED; AND OUR REVENUE-PER-CALL MAXIMIZED. YOU WANT DELSTAR TO CONTINUE TO SEE THE VALUE IN A CENTRALIZED SUPPORT AGENCY; RATHER THAN PLACE CONSIDERATION TOWARDS A VIRTUAL-AGENTED, HOMESOURCED ARCHITECTURE... RIGHT?"

"YES, WE DO. THANK YOU. I WILL RELAY THIS TO MY MANAGERS ON THE GROUND."

"DO WHAT IT TAKES TO GET YOUR WORKFLOW RESOURCE OPTIMIZED."

You almost have to feel sorry for these Service Delivery Director guys – except when you learn how much moolah they rake in. While crappy customers drive *you* mad for a peasley living wage of around $9.50-an-hour; some of those 'director' boys make upwards of $160,000.00 per year for *their* aggravation! Once you learn this fact, your empathy for the Call Center Director flies right out of the fucking window.

...OH BOY...

In the intro, I told you that I know why the caged bird drinks. Well, I also know why *call center workers* drink. They drink to ending another day of talking to **idiotic customers!**

In *DELSTAR*, we were caught smack in the middle of a

war as old as Methuselah, himself. In

One ear everyday, was some customer trying to avoid paying any fees to the bank:

"I DON'T NEED YOU TO TELL ME THAT MY CHECKING ACCOUNT IS IN OVERDRAFT! I ALREADY *KNOW* THAT! WHAT I NEED *YOU* TO TELL ME IS -- HOW COME MY FREAKING *DEBIT CARD* DOESN'T WORK!"

In the other ear everyday, was the bank – trying to avoid providing any freebies to the customer:

"I understand that you have over $3 million dollars in deposits at our bank – and that you feel frustrated, Sir; but you withdrew money from a non-*DELSTAR*, ATM machine; and so the $6 dollar foreign ATM fee will have to apply. I apologize for any inconvenience this may cause."

"NOT AT ALL. I'LL JUST TRANSFER MY $3 MILLION IN DEPOSITS TO

ANOTHER BANK, AND YOU CAN HAVE YOUR SIX DOLLARS."

I mean, the bank emailed us press release after *press release* indicating their new-quarter, 'breakthrough' strategies of generating revenue by-way-of increased deposit fees. Our poor customers were getting

reamed, and we knew it.

"REMEMBER -- IF YOU *CAN* REVERSE A CUSTOMER'S FEE, TELL THEM THAT THE BANK WAS HAPPY TO ASSIST THEM."

"What if we can't... *assist*, I mean."

"IF YOU *CANNOT* REVERSE THE CUSTOMER'S FEES, TELL THEM THAT YOU WERE UNABLE TO REVERSE THE FEE... NOT THE BANK."

I swear to God – if I weren't living in an apartment rental, I would stash every dime I have under my fucking floor boards. Banks suck! Anyway...

...Every now and then, one of us would get a call from somebody

famous.

I remember getting a call from *Addison Seifert*... you know... she used to be on *VideoRotationTV*... now she's on CNC (*CableNewsCast*). So like, ask

me if *I* care! From the time the call began, she was especially mean

to me on the phone! I was shocked – because I was a fan of hers – and I

was going out of my way to be exceptionally helpful to her! To think I

used to watch her on TV all the time! I got my revenge on her

though – because for the rest of that afternoon, I told anyone

who would listen that Addison wasted $968 on clothes at a department store; and she only had $38 left between her checking **and** savings accounts! All that glam on TV and she was flat **broke!** Hmph!

ROTF,

LM

happy Ao!

THERE IS ONE REASON FOR A BANK TO EXIST...

... **A**nd one reason alone. That reason is, for the bank to make money off the backs of the populous. In other words, banks are *seriously* down

with O-P-P...

Yeah, you know me...

See -- most customers who call, say -- a computer company's call center; and speak to their tech support agents, may well be accustomed to grappling with rudeness and communication constraints from overseas agents regarding the setup and operation of the electronic appliances they've just bought. When they call their banking institution however, most normal people have general expectations. They expect that when they call their local bank branch for their bank balance, they will get a person, from their own country, on the other end of the line. Somehow, it feels not only unsettling, but otherworldly – even somewhat *ungodly* -- to have so many personal security checkpoints like passcodes, PIN numbers and verbal identifiers (*like the perennial classic,* MOTHER'S MAIDEN NAME) to be able to access one's own ledger balance; just to hear that balance indifferently chaffed off by the most exaggerated definition of a stranger – a banker who does not even share, or whom may never have seen the currency they are discussing!

I kid you not -- here are some other definitions for the word

stranger, which I found on the Internet; that you can

interchange with mine:

- *Stranger* is **a song** by the rock music group Electric Light Orchestra from their 1983 album Secret Messages. Released as a single in the US.
- *Stranger* was a **band based in Tampa, FL;** formed in the early `80's. They were an extremely-popular band and still worshiped to this day by many fans in Florida, but failed to achieve any real measure of success outside of their home state and southern Georgia.
- *The Stranger* is how the player character of the *Myst* series of games is known in Myst canon.
- *Stranger* was **an enemy of Godzilla** featured in issue sixteen of Dark Horse Comic's "Godzilla King of the Monsters" series.
- *The Stranger* is **a fictional cosmic entity** that appears in the Marvel Universe. The Stranger first appears in Uncanny X-Men vol. 1, #11 (May 1965), and was created by Stan Lee and Jack Kirby.
- **Someone unknown** to the victim.
- *Stalking:* the stalker and the victim do not know each other at all.
- This word generally denotes **a person from a foreign land residing in Palestine.** Such persons enjoyed many privileges in common with the Hebrews, but still were separate from them. The relation of the Hebrews to strangers was regulated by special laws (Deut. 23:3; 24:14-21; 25:5; 26:10-13)...

It all amounts to the same madness:

Anyone (*particularly -- an enemy of Godzilla who may reside in Palestine and plays MYST; with a hit song to his or her credit – as indicated in the definitions above*) **who does not belong in the environment to which they are normally found** – may be on the other end of a customer service call at *DELSTAR;* refusing to reverse bank fees and detachedly doling out deposit balances, day after drudging day.

*D*ELSTAR Bank could care less about how abjectly detestable this concept of *alien-as-personal-accountant* was to its customers. In fact, and for quite some time, the expansion of the bank was no longer through any sort of customer-centric, acquisition of accounts. Rather, the expansion model of the bank for the past 12 or 13 quarters had been to deploy a paradigm shift. They were *full-steam-ahead* into multiple assimilations of smaller banks, investment houses and financial services firms. *DELSTAR* was sucking up companies faster than the *Borg Queen* could get planets assimilated into the COLLECTIVE! *How* fast was that, you ask? Well, when the Banfield site was featured in the bank's corporate newsletter, they couldn't show a single exterior photo of the building. This was because they had been too miserly to pay for new, marquis signage in the front of the building. The sign still showed the name of the previous tenant, CreditCrest!

*A*s for the personal gestures of a bank to make you feel a sense of trust, inter-connectedness and community... LOL! You're kidding, right? Has it occurred to you that the services you have been offered by today's banks encourage isolation and impersonal relations?

It has gone from:

Valued Customer! Come apply for a loan at OUR branch and get a FREE gift !

to:

STAY YOUR LAZY ASS HOME AND APPLY FOR A LOAN ONLINE. WE CAN HANDILY REJECT YOUR LOAN

APPLICATION IN ABOUT 20 SECONDS.

PLUS -- WE CLOSED YOUR BRANCH LAST YEAR -- IN CASE YOU HADN'T NOTICED. WE OFFER MOBILE BALANCE CHECKING AND DIRECT DEPOSIT. WHO NEEDS TO HIRE LIVE TELLERS IN YOUR AREA ?

TRAINING

I GOT OUT OF THE CAB, AND...

There it was -- the *DELSTAR* bank building in Banfield, MO – in all its solid, structural glory.

I stood in the parking lot for a minute to take it all in. The air smelled whiffy fresh, y'know? And the *landscaping*... the landscaping surrounding the parking lot was perfection. I'm not talking about the pristine positioning of the pansies or the precisely patched sections of sod. Rather, the perfection was in the landscape's choking, suffocating, maddening, horticultural reminder that I, *Digital Banker Trainee*, was *Less Than*. Once I walked into that building, I thought, I would officially be classified as a *drone*; an infinitesimal, insignificant

worker-bee – eager to buzz into the bank's vault of confidentiality, credos and customer complaints.

Funny though – for some reason, I walked my dumb-ass up to the main entrance, anyway.

As I looked skyward, from the main entrance of the *DELSTAR* building, it just *hulked* over me and *my* pitiful, little shadow. It was an austere, menacing, brick-and-mortar *behemoth*; intimidating the innocent rookies, like me, and torturing the tired veterans inside with its size, shape, smell and income-generating innuendo.

Fuck it. I need the money, I muttered to myself as I pressed the buzzer on the entry intercom.

"WHO ARE YOU HERE TO SEE?" a forgettable, security guard asked, through the intercom. *I **hate** those things – the intercoms. I can never really hear **what** the other person is saying. Can you?*

"I had an interview with H.R. this morning... "

"OKAY." He sounded like he had the personality of an aerosol can.

As soon as I was buzzed in, I stepped across the ID card-activated threshold of the building. Right away, gargantuan walls of thick, tinted glass had me ambushed in an unrelenting, freezing,

CO_2 recirculating, H-VAC attack! I was *so* cold, and my senses were *so* out-of-sync with my surroundings, that you could have pushed me to the floor with your pointer finger... I mean, I was totally *iced*!

Just beyond the assuming, central lobby and security station, I could hear the whizzing and whirring of the call center's three, main elevators. I surmised straight away, that those elevators were the *True Workhorse Trio* of the call center -- *titanic tributes to OTIS, himself* -- which dipped and dizzied their daily passengers to the harrowing heights and **bottomless depths** of their living-wage lives. I would later learn, that those elevators were the 𝕳𝖔𝖑𝖞 𝕽𝖔𝖑𝖑𝖎𝖓𝖌 𝕿𝖗𝖎𝖓𝖎𝖙𝖞; unabashedly brokering unholy alliances of super-speed, carpet cleaning solvent, stale cigarette tobacco, beat-the-clock sex, home-grown pot and septic-strength, butt-crack.

"HAVE A SEAT. SOMEBODY WILL BE WITH YOU, SHORTLY."

"Thank you," I think I said. I was still pretty cold, but I managed to park my carcass into a *Le Corbusier* inspired, pleather chair. I could tell it was pleather, because there was absolutely NO give. Call center lobbies are renowned the world over, for pretentious displays of cubist discomfort.

Anyhow, I knew that if someone didn't come for me soon, I would petrify where I sat. I mean, how long did they expect me to pretend I was checking my cellphone's push-email? Better yet, how long did they expect me to stare at the clown sitting in the chair across from mine – who was pretending to check *his* push-email?

"You're waiting for HR, too?"

"Yeah," he said, without looking up. I don't know what he was trying to *prove*. One look at his rinky-dink cellphone, and I *knew* that it wasn't capable of receiving push-email. People are so fucking *phony*... whatever.

I had a feeling that what was to come soon would be, more or

less, a battery of mindless assessment tests;

followed by one or two, frivolous interviews with

inept and incessantly irritated on-boarders. I was dead-on.

After about forty minutes of freezing our *kutookusses* off in the lobby, this heavy-set lady, with a long, khaki-colored skirt and scandalously overrun loafers waddled out of the HR office and beckoned us to follow her back inside.

"HAVE EITHER OF YOU EVER WORKED IN A CALL CENTER BEFORE?"

"Can't say that I have," said Mr. Push-email.

I didn't have time to answer stupid questions like that. As soon as we walked into the HR area, I saw a coffee machine and some cups.

FREE COFFEE? That's what *I* wanted to

talk about!

"Hey – is that coffee still hot?"

"YES, BUT IT'S BEEN SITTING THERE SINCE 8:30 THIS MORNING..."

"That's okay," I exclaimed. *Anything* they could do to help me thaw out was a justification for me to work for the company, I thought. Indeed, I was so busy thinking about getting warm that I wasn't paying the least bit of attention to what was going on around me. The HR lady had already seated my lobby colleague at a testing station; and was patiently waiting for me to get my face out of my coffee cup; so she could seat me, as well.

"I'm sorry – it's just that it was *sooo cold* in the hall..." I thought I

 could elicit a little empathy, but I was wrong. The demeanor of the HR representative was even colder than the actual lobby!

"I UNDERSTAND. TAKE A SEAT, PLEASE."

Okay, so I sat down to begin my assessment testing... but I

immediately began freaking out! I mean, gosh! The vast appearance and ambiance of the lobby space had me under the impression that this bank would be equipped with state-of-the-art technology; the best computers, communications systems and peripheral equipment that money could buy! In reality, I was sitting in front of a clunky, old, monochromatic, CRT computer screen; trying to make sense of the DOS-like testing interface – that my grandmother must have used when computers were invented!

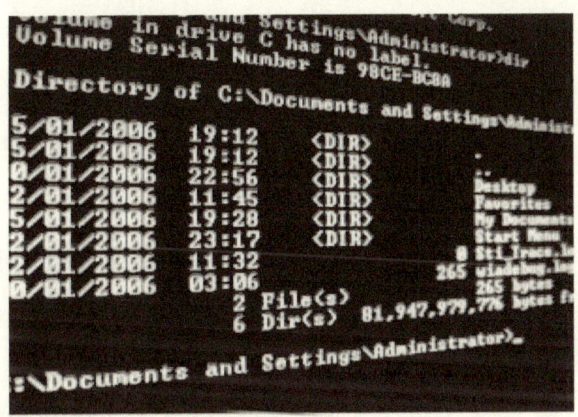

Some of the questions we had to answer were as follows:

- **DO YOU ENJOY MULTITASKING?**

- **HOW IMPORTANT ARE REWARD POINTS IN TODAY'S SOCIETY?**

- **DO YOU BELIEVE PEOPLE SHOULD OWN THEIR OWN HOMES?**

- **SHOULD YOU BE FIRED IF YOU ARE FIVE MINUTES LATE?**

- **IF YOUR COLLEAGUE STEALS A BOX OF PENS, SHOULD YOU REPORT IT TO YOUR MANAGER?**

Did they think anyone was going to answer these questions truthfully?

"Can you believe the nonsense we had to answer?" asked Mr. Push email.

"I'm starting to," I said while trying to fiend some more coffee; "It looks like all you have to be is a US citizen over 18 years of age to get a job here."

After the conclusion of the assessment test,We were both set up for interviews and sent on our separate ways. Crazy though – once I left the building, I simply couldn't get the conceptualization of

Advantage
rewards
Unlock a world of **great benefits**

reward points and

frequent-flyer

miles out of my head! These insidious little things have infected our way of life; becoming a **social standing**

barometer for the hollow brained!

"I chose cash back on my credit card this quarter – because I only have 2,000 reward points."

"*Ouch* -- that's too bad. We actually thought about inviting you to our party next Saturday. Do you have any frequent flyer miles?"

When I checked my email about a week later, I saw one from *DELSTAR*. It was asking me to confirm my interview date and time. This email was also the beginning of an absolutely exasperating,

excruciating and **empty** exchange of

RE: **this** and

RE: RE: **that:**

- Hello Chase,

Thank you for expressing interest in the Digital Banker FT- Banfield class position. We have received your profile and are currently reviewing it.

Please click here if you would like to review your profile.

Please note, your information will be stored in our database and, at this time, will only be matched to jobs in North America, Latin America and Europe. If your experience and qualifications correspond to our requirements, a member of our Workforce Development Network will contact you soon.

We thank you for your interest.

Sincerely,
Debbie Smith
Workforce Development Specialist
DELSTAR Bank – Where the Customer Leads

- Hey, Chase -

I just had a chance to review your application. Thanks for applying for our career opportunity in Digital Banking. Shoot me an email and I will give you all sorts of info on this great career! I look forward to hearing from you; thanks again for your time.

Daria Alvarez
Recruiter
DELSTAR Digital Banking

- Hello, Daria --

I appreciate your email. I'd love to hear more about the opportunity! Some people I know work at *DELSTAR*, and they have both encouraged me to go for it! LOL

Yours Truly,

Chase

- Hi Debbie!

I'd like to thank you for your patience and time on the phone with me this afternoon. It was my pleasure to speak with you.

You mentioned that Daria Alvarez would be getting in touch with me. As it turns out; when I logged in to Yahoo to send you this email, there was an email in my box from her!

Thank you so much. If I am hired at *DELSTAR*, I will make a point to meet you in person!

Yours Truly,

Chase

- Chase -

I am excited that you are interested. I have a class starting on the 18th of September. The schedule can range between having a start time from 11AM to 12PM and ending between 8PM to 9PM - 4 days a week and one weekend day. The first four weeks of employment you are in training which goes M-F from 8:30AM-5:30PM. Starting wage is $9.50/hour. Let me know if you are still interested and I can have you complete your compatibility assessment.

Daria Alvarez
Recruiter
DELSTAR Digital Banking

- **By All Means, Daria --**

I would be delighted to participate in any sort of prerequisite activity you may require.

I look forward to receiving your instructions.

Best Regards,

Chase

- **Hi Chase -**

We would need you to assess for the position. We are here 9-4 M-F; Stop by our offices and let the Guards know you are here to take an assessment. nce in the HR office, tell them you are there to take the DIGITAL BANKER assessment. Thanks.

Daria Alvarez
Recruiter
DELSTAR Digital Banking

- **Dear Chase:**

We are pleased to present our offer for you to join *DELSTAR* Bank! We are delighted at the prospect of your joining the firm.

This letter contains the entire understanding between us. The specifics of the offer are:

Position:
•DIGITAL BANKER
•Banfield, MO
•Work Schedule: Any 5 of the 7 days of the week 11/12PM-8/9PM, after training is completed.*

Compensation:
• Annual Base pay of $19,760.00

Benefits:
•You will receive a Benefits Sign-up Kit within the first 10 days after starting work, which will provide you with details about how to make your benefit selections. You will also be able to review this information on the *DELSTAR* Bank corporate Intranet approximately 72 hours after your start date.

Beginning Work:
•Critical instructions on completing new hire forms and information for us to complete your background check will be sent to you shortly via email. It is important that you complete the forms immediately. Failure to comply with this request could delay your start date or may cause us to rescind our offer. In addition, it is important that you complete your fingerprinting and drug testing . If you need assistance, please reply to this email with your request.

Employment Tender:
•Your offer of employment is subject to satisfactory completion of all pre-employment processing, including a background check, fingerprint processing, drug screening, anal probe and your completion of all forms necessary for employment.

•Your first 90 days on the job will be an introductory period. During the introductory period, you or your manager may terminate your employment if he or she determines that you are not appropriately qualified and/or suited for the position. You will remain an employee-at-will at all times."Employee-at-will" means that either you or the company may terminate your employment at any time, for any or no reason.
•You must read and understand the company Rules of Conduct prior to joining the company..

We are very excited at the prospect of your joining our team!

Please indicate your acceptance by replying to this email in the affirmative.

Sincerely,

Daria Alvarez
DELSTAR Bank - Digital Banking Staffing

BORED YET? I HEAR 'YA. HAVE YOU EVER SEEN ANYTHING SO FUTILE?

Anyway, once they let me know that I was in;

Your offer of employment is subject to satisfactory completion of all pre-employment processing, including a background check, fingerprint processing, drug screening, anal probe and your completion of all forms necessary for employment.

that I was going to be an indentured servant;

Annual Base pay of $19,760.00

who they could fire-at-will...

You will remain an employee-at-will at all times. "Employee-at-will" means that either you or the company may terminate your employment at any time, for any or no reason.

that's all I needed.

I was so excited!

START GATE

The more advanced a company's website is, you will find a direct proportion to how primitive their training processes and training materials are. Certificates-of-Completion for training are no longer meticulously fashioned and printed on heavyweight, cream-colored card stock; to be signed by hand. These days, and especially in call centers, course completion certificates are xeroxed by the ream-loads from black-only, ink-jet printers.

This proportional equation of advanced corporate website to primitive training curriculum is most readily evidenced by the forced viewing of dumbed down, mind numbing **PowerPoints**.

Bill Gates has **got** to be dismayed by the **thousands-**

upon-thousands of left-justified text blocks that have

passed themselves off as corporate, educational training presentations in

recent years. Check this one out...

Slide #1 -

YOU ARE A DIGITAL BANKER

-

A GUARDIAN of DEPOSITS

Slide #2 -

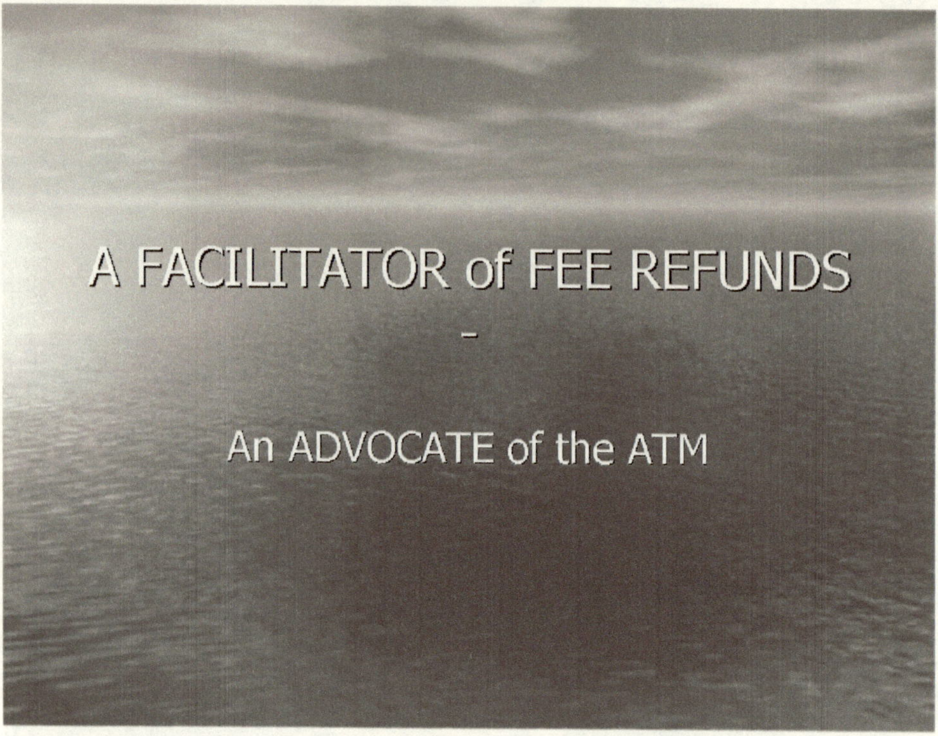

A FACILITATOR of FEE REFUNDS

–

An ADVOCATE of the ATM

You CAJOLE the Customer
with

COMPASSION, CONCERN and
RAPPORT

You FINANCE the Customer
with

FEE-BASED, USER-FRIENDLY
SOLUTIONS

O_ur trainer was a lady named, Bronwyn Callaghan. I miss Bronwyn. I didn't know what to make of her at first; but I loved her at the end. She looked just *like* Hillary Clinton – except her hair was a little less red – no, it was red; a lighter red. She dressed much dowdier than Hillary; but she had the *same* face. Bronwyn laughed a lot. She had a tendency to go off on various tangents about her personal life, though. I couldn't figure out whether it was to establish authority in the classroom, or just to fill time; or maybe, to form some sort of connection with the group.... or what. Fact *was*, she would go off on these rants ...

... giving *way* too much information about stuff like:

- her personal romantic *preferences*; and
- her children's various and vacant excursions to countless *ballparks*;
- where she saw them make a bunch of home *runs*; and
- she served sandwiches and sodas and fries and franks to the *kids*; and
- courageously carpooled to those ballgames with any random assemblage of *parents*; who
- would hiss in insane fits of jealousy over the miraculous athletic achievements of her angelic *kids*; who
- *hated* having to socialize and be nice to any of her personal romantic *preferences*; and
- getting dragged to all the various and vacant excursions to countless *ballparks*;
- where they were sick-to-death of hitting hapless home *runs*; and
- carpooling to their ballgames with random assemblages of moronic kids and their equally childish *parents*; who
- never offered their mother a *dime* towards her $4-per-gallon *gas* ...

...Bronwyn was an excellent trainer. As long as you were a participant in her training class, she was fixated on your success. Once you left the training though, there may well be times when she'd look you dead in your face without speaking. It wasn't because she performing any sort of slight against you, or anything;, it was because she was in her OWN zone – that's the best way I can describe it. Bronwyn gave one hundred percent of herself to everything that she did. This was evidenced by the fact that most of the time when you passed by her cubicle, you could look inside (3-*sided*) and see her with her back towards you on her speakerphone in a teleconference; with a piece of string blocking her cubicle's entry. The string would have a piece of paper dangling from the middle like a shirt on a clothesline. It would read something to the effect of: **MEETING IN PROGRESS** -- or some other some such.

For our part, the entire month-long training program was an irritating and incidental hurdle to receiving an answer to the burning question:

WHEN DO WE GET OUR FIRST PAYCHECK?

Answers to that, or any other question the class felt collectively compelled to know were dangled on deliberately woven strings of angst, anticipation and vacuously vocalized verbiage like:

"WE DON'T KNOW, YET..."

"WE'LL HAVE TO LOOK INTO IT..."

"WE'RE STILL TRYING TO FIND OUT FROM CORPORATE..."

Such tactical maneuvers as this willful withholding of paycheck and commission payout information from trainees is intended to perform the same set of functions as the *planned silence* moment at a job interview. In that case, hiring managers are handbook-bound to sigh, then create an awkward, asynchronous pause as they suggest:

"TELL ME A LITTLE ABOUT YOURSELF..."

The theory is that if they remain silent and stare at you like you're crazy, you will inadvertently seek to end your feeling of awkwardness and discomfort by running your mouth and revealing something candid, unasked, and absurd. *This is a textbook form of intimidation.*

So – by not giving call center trainees any inkling as to what salary they will actually make -- or when they can look forward to their first monetary reward hitting the palm of their hands – these training departments have deployed the insidious application of hierarchical structure upon the class. At *DELSTAR,* this structure is built on the three-tiered foundation that, simply put, is this:

. THE BANK COMES FIRST.

. YOU ARE A PION.

. YOUR PAY FOR HOURS WORKED IS INCIDENTAL.

Ain't *that* some shit.

Hmph. I thought the whole idea was the most

SDRAWKCAB SSA thing I'd ever *heard* of! I don't know

about you, but the last time *I* checked, knowing what date *I* would be

paid served as an **excellent** motivator for *me* to continue to contribute

my time, energy, skills and labor to a corporate entity. Having no clue

about when I would get paid or what amount?

Nnnnnnn... not so much.

ROLL CALL

One of the first things Bronwyn did when our *Digital Banker* training began, was make all of us introduce ourselves to each other. It was like being in a **TRAINEES ANONYMOUS** meeting. We went around the whole room, like six-year-olds; telling everybody the most bizarre things about ourselves:

"Hi. I'm *Cherise*."

Cherise went first. She was the only black person in my training class, besides Osazogbenowan; who we called Benny .

Being the Queen Ant in our sack of white flour didn't seem to bother Cherise, as least on the surface.

If it was me, I would bother me a lot. I was glad that she didn't trip about it, though. I mean, it was kind of obvious that African-Americans at *DELSTAR*, and in Banfield, still weren't getting 100 percent of the opportunities they were entitled to; and that fact in-and-of-itself is fucked up about our country, as a whole. I do know that Cherise was smarter that at least three of the rest of us put together! Racism sucks.

In fact, seeing a black person *anywhere* in the neighborhood around the bank was as exciting as spotting the *Loch Ness Monster*, or finding **AREA 51**. Even *she* would get excited at the prospect!

"Ooh, lookie loo," Cherise would say to me if we were outside on break and we saw a black person walking by the bank; "Itsa *black peepis!*" she knew I hated that shit... but I knew she was right.

"Shut up, Cherise! You're so silly."

If you want the truth, I believe that the African-Americans in Banfield had an unspoken way of communicating between themselves. They would always acknowledge the other's presence, somehow, or the other;

without being noticed by the public, at-large.

Maybe it was the special and quiet way they nodded their heads when they passed each other by in the halls. Or, like, it might have even been a certain eye gesture, or off-kilter hum none of us white people could put our fingers on. Anyway, you could tell that Cherise was was proud to see her people, 'representing' on the phones at *DELSTAR*; even though it was a job where none of the customers would ever see their faces.

"Hi. I'm *Langley*."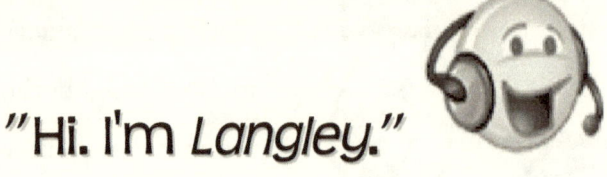

Langley went next. She was a stunning beauty, both inside and out. She had great skin, shampoo-commercial hair and reflective eyes that allowed you to peer right through to her gentle soul. She was the poster-child for natural beauty. Unfortunately, she had no conception of the kind.

I don't know what her home life was like – other than the fact that she had a son in preschool. What I *did* know was that her home

environment was doing **nothing whatsoever** to support her self-esteem.

She wore the dowdiest clothing, too. She would come to work in stuff like cream colored, windbreaker jackets and long, flounced skirts with alternate rows of the drabbest cabbage-rose fabric and panels of

cheap lace. I realize that we were in Missouri; but even Laura

Ingalls Wilder, were she

alive today, may like to take an occasional trip to *Macy's*, or something... you

think?

To everyone's surprise, Langley left *DELSTAR* after only two days on the floor. She was the first one of our class to quit.

"Um... I'm *Kayleigh*."

Kayleigh was *beautiful* – inside and out. She had smooth, brown skin and the shiny, black hair of a 'coolie gal'. She had an ear-to-ear smile like Barack Obama's and a personality to boot; but she was -- hands down --

the dizziest person in the group. I wish I'd gotten to know her better. She invited me to be her friend on *PageSpace* and she was always sending me messages and leaving delightful little snippets and comments on my page. Two or three days after she met me for the first time in training class, Kayleigh sent me the *coolest* text message! It read:

> **CABLE NEWS CAST reports a retard**
> **escaped from a mental home.**
> **1 million dollar reward.**
> **U know I love you but I need the money.**
> **Where the fuck r u?**

"I'm Alexandra."

Alexandra was a fool. She said she'd lost her previous job by traveling across country with some man. Apparently, this man left her with a toddler who was still in diapers; and pregnant with another child. She also smoked during her pregnancy and justified it by saying that she wasn't going to keep the baby.

"Alex, you know in your first trimester you're not supposed to go near anything that begins with a letter C -- no cola, no caffeine, no cats, no candy, no *cigarettes*..."

"Yeah, I know. But I'm not keeping the baby – so it doesn't make any difference."

Alexandra could usually be spotted with a vitamin-enhanced water in one hand and a cigarette in the other. I didn't get it. To me, it was like the people you see who order a quintuple cheese deluxe burger with a diet cola.

"Okee dokee... "

She was about the stupidest bitch in the call center; but it wasn't *my* baby – what was I supposed to do? Call child services so they could take her other baby? No; but what I *did* do was stop talking to her.

When you hurt kids... this kind of thing just rubs me the wrong way.

"Hello. I'm *Rachelle.*"

"This is the best job I've ever had in my life."

"GREAT! WELCOME TO *DELSTAR*," said Bronwyn.

Rachelle used to work as a cashier in a convenience store; on the outskirts of the city. As such, she was determined to keep her entry-level job on the *DELSTAR* floor; even if it meant foregoing promotions to higher-paying positions. It seemed to me, like she was on some kind of **personal quest** to prove to herself that she could do more with her life than ring up cigarettes, six-packs and lotto tickets at the corner, convenience mart... Only, she was too **unskilled and unmotivated** to do much else, I think.

I sincerely liked Rachelle and admired her resolve; I just didn't have any inkling about how to **communicate** with her. Nobody did. If we were in the break room together, for example, she would just start saying the most depressing **stuff** – out of the clear blue sky:

"I **hate** my sonofabitch ex-husband."

"I'm sorry... well... do you have any kids?"

"My eldest daughter is a recovering addict. She got to using that

meth, and whatnot."

"I'm sorry, Rachelle... well... do you have any OTHER kids?"

"I just won a custody fight to take my grandson away from my

son's miserable **ex-wife**; because she got into that **meth**

stuff, too."

It was hopeless trying to get Rachelle to lighten up.

"Whaddup. I'm

Jackson."

"TELL US ABOUT YOURSELF, JACKSON," said Bronwyn.

"Uuuhhh-- I'm into **CUBICLE**; and so like, that's pretty

much it. Oh – and I *love* the

Green Bay Packers!

Dum ^{di} dum -

^{di} dum dum dum dum - Go, Pack, Go!"

Jackson was a **CUBICLE** junkie. Remember that movie, **CUBICLE**? It was a hit in the nineties; about the guy who hated his office job. Maybe you don't remember, but *Jackson* sure did. He had the *mug*... the *t-shirt*... the *bendable, laptop computer action figure* that opened and shut... *He even had the famous,* royal-blue staple gun! It was ridiculous! I hate that movie, now. I liked Jackson just fine, but every time I passed his desk, I wanted to staple him in the head with his own staple gun; then burn down the building.

"Hey. I'm *Cookie*."

Cookie was chill. She was fat, but she was an accomplished makeup artist with the most bewitching, greenish-yellowish eyes. I'm not gay, but I couldn't help staring at her face like I was a groupie when she was around!

"When I'm not working, I like to play the bass," she said to the class.

"ROCK OUT, FRET-FREAK!" Bronwyn exclaimed.

Cookie was indeed, a big **fret-freak**; who seized every opportunity she could, to play bass guitar and color a conversation with sexual innuendos. I don't blame her, though. I mean – there's something about a great bassline that makes me want to fuck, too...

Men, batteries... Who cares *what* you're humping on when the **bass** is groovin'! **LOLOL** Anyway, Cookie is on *PageSpace* like most of the class – but we never got around to exchanging pages.

"Hi. I'm *Cassandra.*"

At first I wasn't sure **what** to make of Cassandra – then I understood. She was even more insecure and unsure of herself than I was of myself! Her hands were unsteady and she couched her breasts in her arms to pronounce them to you – as more of a habit than out of vanity. She was really a doll, once you got to know her. I believe she may have been molested as a child; by a family member. I mean, she showed all the signs... she seemed entirely **preoccupied** with catching eye of the men on the call center floor. She seemed to have some kind of food allergy, too. One day, she ate an eggroll from the cafeteria; and three hours later she was in the emergency room. I heard she was upset because she couldn't access her *PageSpace* page from her hospital bed.

"Hey. I'm *Joseph.*"

T hen there was **Joseph**. He was nice enough; but he was

unnaturally attached... okay... he was **hopelessly**

addicted to the TV show, **36**. That's the series where the whole season is supposed to take place in 36, real-time hours. I guess you could say his entire life revolved around a day-and-a-half of

everyone else's.

"Hi. I'm *Darcy.*"

Darcy was a smart, unsophisticated biker chick who belonged in the seventies.

"This whole thing is stupid, Bronwyn. Are these name tags necessary?"

"HUMOR ME, DARCY; JUST HUMOR ME," Bronwyn replied as she turned to the class;. NAME TAGS ARE FUN, PEOPLE – WHETHER WE LIKE IT, OR NOT."

I knew that Darcy was my kind of friend, because she had a plaque on her desk that said,

THERE IS NOTHING MORE DEMORALIZING THAN A SMALL, BUT ADEQUATE INCOME

How cool is that! Too bad Darcy couldn't stand *me*. She hated my guts.

" I'm *Debbie,* y'all."

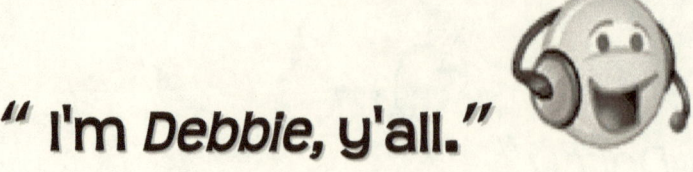

Debbie was sweet, southern and suffocating. Every day of training, she brought in a box of donuts or blueberry muffins for the class.

"My husband was assigned to security guard detail for

Susan MacDougal - back in the nineties - when she was in prison. Y'all remember Susan MacDougal, right?"

Debbie had only moved to town in the past month. I liked her for sure; but I didn't see us becoming super close. She struck me as one of those adorably simple, well meaning types who pronounce the word,

insurance with emphasis on the first syllable – 'INsurance' (*That*

annoys the shit *out of me... but people in the Heartland pronounce the*

word, insurance like that... all the time. *For some reason, the same people add a third syllable to the word,* nuclear, *as well. To them, the*

word is nū-cu-lurrr *; and that's all there is* to *it!*).

"I always dreamed that one day, I would get rich and own a big house in the Hamptons,"she told us one day, at lunch. Didn't we *all*. LOL

"The **Hamptons?**" Jackson shrieked; "You probably don't even keep the pool clean that you've got in your backyard

now!"

Jackson was right; though he didn't know it at the time. Since then,

several of the girls on the floor have been to **Debbie's**

house, and they've seen her backyard. By all unanimous account

and accord, Debbie's swimming pool is disgusting.

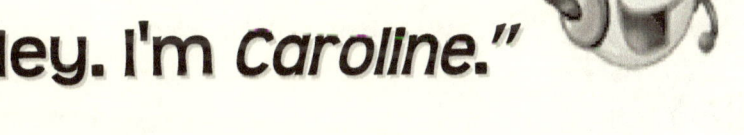

"Hey. I'm *Caroline*."

Caroline was older... I guess, like, in her late forties, or in that

area. She was recently remarried; to a younger man who

has a couple of kids.

I was **constantly** laughing when I was around Caroline! It was so funny -- because her cellphone was always going off at indiscriminate moments. And -- that wasn't even the **worst** part! If she got a call from one of her kids, her ringtone was the theme from *Sesame Street*. We knew if her husband called, because *I Don't Want No Scrubs* would come on. If one of her side dishes phoned in, we would hear, *It's Raining Men...* Hallelujah.

Caroline was a little more sophisticated than the rest of the girls in my training class. She had a keen interest in *home furnishings*; especially in the pieces which had historical references. When I wasn't teasing her about **robbing the cradle**, she would always try to school me in the ways of interior design.

"Ooh, Chase! There was this crystal piece I spotted on bidBaY," she would say.

"Yeah? Fantastic! Is it an antique?"

"I think it's a piece from the early-to-mid, ART~NEO~CLASSI^WHATNOT^DECOICAL~ROQUE~WAVE period. I'd have to check the pedigree online."

God love her – period antiques meant as much to me while I was working at *DELSTAR* as a scratched-off lottery ticket means to

you, right now: **absolutely nothing.**

"*Roman* here."

Roman was married to one of the ladies who worked in the cafeteria. He was jazz loving white trash from Denver; a laid-back underachiever and super cool dude. He was the guy I was sitting next

to in the lobby when I first applied for the job... remember? **Mr.**

push email.

How Roman advanced within the company, **I'll never**

know; except to say that he is **living proof** that call centers reward mediocre performance. I mean, laid back? My man was

laid back to the point of **narcolepsy!** Last I heard, he'd been

promoted twice; and found a comfortable spot in the

107

email division. He never sold a damned thing to *anyone* – yet he got

pushed right up through the ranks, to the cushie

comfort of the email unit.

A WORD ABOUT THE EMAIL UNIT

To work in the email division of *DELSTAR* was
to be assured of a permanent job until you
retired. It was where call center reps went to
die. You could put on a pair of headphones,
listen to your favorite CDs and type fee
refund rejection letters all the live-long
day! The email system was called, MANA; we
called it MANA FROM HEAVEN.

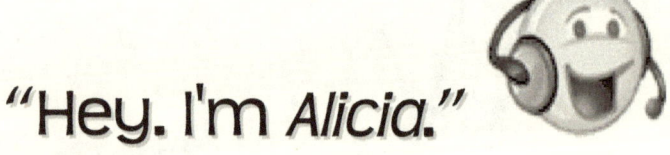

"Hey. I'm *Alicia.*"

Alicia was adorable. Besides being known for her pleasantness and

cute smile, she ended up having the best adherence in the entire call

center. She was always at her desk! I don't know how she

pulled it off!

We called her *Rosie Rainbow*. Have you ever seen her cubicle? It was

a goddamned psychedelic shack! Everything was rainbow

colored... the *gel pens*. The *mug*. The *mousepad*. The *hard candies*...

...I *knew* when she showed up in training one day with rainbow-

colored sticky notes -- that we were gonna be in for it when

she hit the floor and got her own desk.

"Okay, so, I'm *Iris*."

I was crazy about Iris from the minute she first

opened her mouth. She was the most lovable, hypochondriac;,

chain-smoking talkaholic I had ever met! Once our class got on the call

center floor, Iris was just loaded with stories about her retarded

boyfriend, Ralston; the five million reasons we should find her some

Percocet and her abhorrently miserable customers!

"Hey, Chase! Last night, I dreamed that I was impaling one of my
customers in the eye with the stylus of my PDA."

"What?"

Ralston lived with Iris; and he worked on the floor, too. He didn't say much – but he didn't really have to. Iris kept us all filled in.

"Ralston is SUCH an asshole. The other night, I let him use my laptop – and now I can't get my stupid WIRELESS to work! I SO cannot SURF, at this point! And so, like -- What the F?"

Three months after we hit the floor, Iris quit the job due to illness. As it turns out, she wasn't just a chain-smoking hypochondriac – she was *really sick.* I was petrified at the prospect!

"Hello, all. I'm *Jillian.*"

Aah. Jillian. She was very smart, but she had a completely **treacherous** habit of throwing her intelligence in everybody's face. Most of us wanted to punch her

squarely in hers.

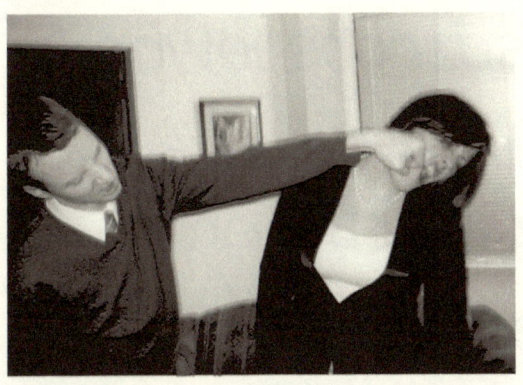

A curious thing happened, though. After about four

months out of training, Jillian began to change her hair and manner of

dress to a much more mature, attractive and professional level.

Next thing I knew, she became the nicest person on the

whole floor! It was like watching *Ebenezer Scrooge* transform from a

grumpy, old geezer into a giddy and generous gentleman!

Along with Alicia, Jillian shared the best adherence in the call

center. She had a page on *PageSpace,* as well. I checked it out and

thought it was decent; but I don't think she ever got around to

uploading her photo on her page. Through all her posturing,

111

Jillian was extremely insecure about herself. It's a shame because she had absolutely, no reason to be.

"I am *Osazogbenowan.*"

We liked to call him, Benny. Benny from Benin.

"Osa-socked-Benjamin... what the heck does your name **mean**, man?"

"It means, **God chooses the right place..**"

"YOU **KNOW** WE CAN'T PRONOUNCE THAT CRAZY NAME OVER HERE IN AMERICA, RIGHT?" On occasion, Bronwyn could be amazingly *insensitive.*

"I know. We cannot pronounce it in Benin, either. Just call me Benny."

Benny came to the USA from the African country of Benin. He tried to escape poverty and sub-Saharan culture but his **entire African family** followed him to the US. Sometimes you could see the strain of housing his whole family in his apartment, on his face when he came to work.

Benny said he didn't have a girlfriend; but he was joined at the hip

with **Cookie and Alicia** during breaks. I think he was

fucking Cookie on the side, actually.

Rumor was, that Benny from Benin had a

swanson johnson!

I *believe* it, too — even the geographical outline of
the country of Benin makes it look like a
hugerrific, thrusteronomous johnson! Check it out:

DAY TWO

O n the second day of training, the Environmental Services representative came to talk to the class. Boy, was she hardcore! This lady was a butch on the edge of an emphysema diagnosis.

"I DON'T WORK FOR *DELSTAR* – I WORK FOR *BUILDING SERVICES* (cough). IF I CATCH YOU DEFACING ANY ROOM OR FURNITURE ON THIS PROPERTY, I WILL HAVE YOU SENT DOWNTOWN ON MISDEMEANOR CHARGES."

You had to wonder if her living room was full of cheap furniture from those closeout liquidators who saturated the Missouri airwaves with weekly assaults of the most pestering TV commercials....

...come on down to **PROPERTY LIQUIDATION WAREHOUSE!**

We'll leave the light on so you can shop 'till you drop!

*...You **tell'em**, Harlan!*

Building Security also had *their* turn to torture and

terrorize the class during training. Grace, the Chief of Security, was also, a fifty-ish, short haired, butch-bitch; but I'll have to say that even *she* was less hardcore than the Mack Truck from Facilities

Management! Yeesh! Grace made sure to highlight every last one of the other six million things we were not allowed to do that the Facilities lady may have neglected to mention in her previous fear-mongering session.

"AS FAR AS THIS BUILDING'S CONCERNED, THE BUCK STOPS WITH *ME*," said Grace as her eyes caressed the contours of a girl in the back of the room's blouse. She was revolting. I could see why she was hired for security. Her eyes weren't missing *shit*. I didn't really listen to the rest of the

security spit she was spewing; but as my mind slowly slapped against each of the four ceiling corners of the

training room like Atari Pong, I could've *sworn* I heard her say, "BASICALLY, IT'S OUR JOB TO RIDE YOU, BELITTLE YOU AND GENERALLY, MAKE YOU FELL LIKE YOU ARE CONSTANTLY UNDER SUSPICION WHILE YOU ARE WORKING HERE AT *DELSTAR*. ANY QUESTIONS?"

DAY THREE

Activity ID	Activity Description	Early Start	Early Finish	2003	2004	2005	2006	2007	2008
+ SITE PREPARATION									
		04NOV03	31AUG04						
MAIN EXHIBITION BUILDING									
2043	Drill Caissons @ Area 3	03MAR04	30JUL04						
2015	Drill Caissons @ Area 2	15APR04	15JUN04						
2000	F/R/P Shallow Foundations @ Area 3	05MAY04	07OCT04						
2220	Underground Utilities Inside Building	05MAY04	02FEB05						
2020	F/R/P Shallow Foundations @ Area 2	15JUN04	12AUG04						
2025	Drill Caissons @ Area 1	15JUN04	14OCT04						
2030	F/R/P Shallow Foundations @ Area 1	17AUG04	15JAN05						
2035	Erect/Detail Structural Steel @ Area 3	01SEP04	29APR05						
2045	Erect/Detail Structural Steel @ Areas 2, 1, & 4	01SEP04	01NOV05						
2045	Drill Caissons @ Area 4	19OCT04	16MAR05						
2070	Prep & Pour Slab On Deck	05DEC04	08MAR05						
2055	F/R/P Shallow Foundations @ Area 4	16DEC04	15JUL05						
2076	Spray On Fireproofing	04FEB05	05MAY05						
2090	Install Mechanical Systems	09MAR05	05FEB07						
2091	Install Electrical Systems	09MAR05	05FEB07						
2093	Install Plumbing Systems	09MAR05	05FEB07						
2094	Install Fire Protection Systems	09MAR05	05FEB07						
2096	Install Exterior Skin	08APR05	01DEC05						
2005	Prep & Pour Slabs On Grade	03MAY05	28OCT05						
2100	Install Roofing	05MAY05	31OCT05						
2476	Prep & Pour Topping Slabs	05JUN05	05APR06						
2105	Install Elevators & Escalators	05JUN05	05JUN07						
2110	Interior Finishes	05JUN05	31OCT07						
2092	Central Plant Mechanical/Electrical Rooms	27OCT05	28SEP07						
2120	Punch List	01FEB07	31MAR08						
2115	Landscaping & Street Work	01MAR07	30NOV07						
+ EXISTING GARAGE & CONFERENCE CENTER									
		02DEC03	28JUL05						
+ PLATT FACADE RELOCATION									
		13OCT02	19OCT04						
+ ELEVATED SERVICE ROADWAY & LOADING DOCK PLAZA									
		07MAY04	09OCT05						
+ EXTERIOR UTILITIES									
		28JAN04	15JUN05						
+ PYLONS									
		15JUL05	14MAR06						
+ BUILDING CONTROLS CONNECTIONS									
		01SEP05	05JUN06						

Sheet 1 of 1

On the third day of training, we had a teleconference with the bank's scheduling department. They were based in Marietta, Georgia. Their entire reason for living was to calculate and compound the seconds any call center agent dared to be out of adherence. We sat for two hours; nodding like jolly junkies while the girl from Georgia recited a litany of southern-fried instructions to us – regarding the slides we were supposed to be looking at in our room while she talked.

117

We had a system called, *iPlanitScheduler* (*part of the larger, INPECT Human Capital Management System*); which a lot of call centers used. *DELSTAR* deployed it with a self-service interface. Employees could put in their preferred shifting bids; and receive a scheduled response from within one-half hour to 24 hours after their bid was entered into the system. Employees would learn of bid approvals or rejections through emailed responses from the Georgia scheduling team. The employee's schedule outline in the *iPlanitScheduler* system would also be updated, accordingly.

Our class already knew that we had to work through Christmas unless the call center was closed; because in order to get a Christmas off, you would have had to but your shift bid into *iPlanitScheduler* at least a

year and a-half in advance. We had been there for two days; and had not yet been trained on how to use the system.

The systems we had to learn in training besides the *iPlanitScheduler* were the scheduling systems, the customer relationship management system (ours was called, UNIKRASH); the VoiP (Internet phone) system and the bank's corporate Intranet – which included real-time updated, corporate reference materials. Every copy of every informational and marketing piece issued by *DELSTAR* would be posted on this Intranet in PDF form; but since we weren't allowed to use the printers, we could never print the damned PDF documents out. We weren't allowed to make copies of these documents, either. We were also, not allowed to take our training materials home – to study them and try to retain any of the information we were trained. Evidently, we were all on some sort of singular mission to ship vast amounts of sales scripts to AL QAEDA.

Anyway, since we were not allowed to fax anything to anyone, either, procedures which required receipt of End User (customer) information via-fax, were a bewildering and cataclysmic event! To get such permission, you had to choose between chasing down a manager who wasn't available -- or -- humiliating yourself in front of a manager who didn't like you.

In training, our desks hugged three of the four walls of the room; while a dry-erase board spanned the length of the remaining wall. Everybody in the class would swirl around, in our gas-lifted, office chairs; keeping our backs to the desks for the greater part of the day. This was so we could watch Bronwyn and her assistants fumble with overhead projectors and busted audio speakers every day. The equipment sat on a rolling cart; and by the time they got the speakers and the projector working in tandem with Bronwyn's computer, one of

119

them would forget the **password** they needed to login to the training presentations! We never learned *anything* in class until after our first, daily break! ROTFLOMAO!

Right behind the 'techno-gizmo' cart, we had a large, round, grey-flecked, melamine activity table. I felt like I was in third grade. At any time, six or seven chairs could wheel up to the table; or I suppose, 13 or 14 of us could gather around it, if we *had* to.

The tabletop was always full. Industrial sized, emptied and half-cut, bottles of bleach or jars of mayonnaise; which were filled and overflowing with markers, crayons and dried-up highlighters (*third grade, remember?*). At times, people would bring bags of candy or boxes of assorted *Sticky Kreem* donuts and dump them like so much litter, in the middle of the table.

One day, Bronwyn had us perform some kind of training exercise with massive pieces of *Stickit-note* paper. I thought this stuff only came in those little pad-squares; but this paper was poster sized! On this paper, we were each supposed to interpret how we envisioned our lives five years out; how we saw ourselves at *DELSTAR*, and whatnot. Some people would draw stick figures; some people would write letters or memos – and place random words all over their page. A couple of people would pretend that they were in art school and draw over every inch of their paper; some other people would **resort to dumb shit** like placing a solitary dot at a random point on their page – or – creating a solitary, uneven, marker blot for pseudo-intellectual 'shock' value. Others would complain about how **obtuse** they thought the whole exercise to be.

When our posters were done, Bronwyn had us put them up on the wall space over our desks; leaving them as personal identifiers. A few of the girls in the class began trading tiny, multicolored *Stickit-notes* between each other when Bronwyn's back was turned. If someone received a note, they would stick it to their 'identity' poster as and expansion of their art-scape and a symbol of their popularity within the class.

Turns out that the black girl, Cherise, got so many notes from the girls that you couldn't even see what she drew on her paper after awhile. The *stickits* were exercises themselves – in general **boredom**; and they would say the most ludicrous stuff like,

- *What are you doing Thursday?*
- *Send me a note back...*
- *So-and-so has been talking about you behind your back. You should watch out for her.*

TELE-PATRIOTS

In training, we learned many things about facets of State and Federal banking regulations, processes and procedures. One of the most notable

things we learned was the **USA PATRIOT ACT:**

Uniting and

Strengthening

America by

Providing

Appropriate

Tools

Required to

Intercept and

Obstruct

Terrorism

Another one of the most notable things we learned was the influence of radical, ISLAMIC culture on the state of American Banking. Apparently,

OSAMA BIN-LADEN has a particular interest in the lives of poor, insignificant, call-center employees living in the Ozarks. By the time we were through learning the regulatory aspects of our jobs, we were clear about the fact that :

- We would **never** wire any amount of money to anyone over one-

  hundred dollars, *ever again*... lest we get banished to

the hills of AFGHANISTAN – along with the rest of AL QAEDA...

- If we came to work with USB flash drives on our keychains, stainless-steel silverware (*from home*) for our lunch or cameras on our cellphones, we would be escorted off the premises and banished to the hills of AFGHANISTAN – along with the rest of AL QAEDA...

- The last ten people who were fired from the *DELSTAR* Bank call center were escorted off the premises and banished to the hills of AFGHANISTAN – along with the rest of AL QAEDA. Evidently, the Afghan hills are alive with cyber-hacking hillbillies and high-tech rednecks – who are **all**

out of adherence...

- We would be held *personally* responsible if – through some manner of reverse fiscal osmosis -- AL QAEDA got their hands on the deposit accounts of our countless, credit-crunched corral of boorish and indigent customers; who owed kablillions of dollars in noncollectable and returned check fees to the bank. In which case, we would, most assuredly, be be escorted off the premises and banished to the hills of AFGHANISTAN – along with the rest of AL QAEDA...

TRANSITION

At the halfway point in training, Bronwyn moved us to a **new**

room. In this room (*which some call centers call 'bridge', 'transition', 'ramp' or 'driver's ed'*), the objective was to take calls from actual customers – under the supervision of a handful of 'helpers'; trainee assistants. Some people called the second-level support, training helpers, monitors, support technicians; etc.. Whatever these guys were called, they only made one dollar more per hour than we did. The way they belittled and ignored the trainees in the transition room though; you would think they were being paid twice the floor agent's salary! I mean, they

knew they had you in a bind – because everything you did for or said to a customer in the transition room – had to be approved by one of them, first. You couldn't provide the customer with a solution without their authorization; you couldn't end the call without their authorization;

so you and your customer got jacked.

I believe the assistant trainers took exceptional pride in making you wait twenty minutes (*with your hand stuck in the air*) for help; all day, every day; through the entire transitional training period. I found these junior trainees to be some of the most discourteous, most nonchalant,

disaffected individuals I've just about *ever* had the pleasure of meeting! Maybe they were technically proficient, but the *people* skills were nowhere to be found! Moreover, don't expect them to speak to you *whatsoever*, once you leave the training environment. Why should they?

After all – they make a whole dollar more than *you* do, remember?

At first, I had the impression that it may be of some career advantage to become an assistant trainee, down the line – like, after I was on the floor for a little while. When I examined the *faces* of the assistants we had in our transition period, though; I noticed that they all seemed to

behave as the most miserable, misanthropic set of

IGORIAN GIMPS; in the throes of

some medieval, colossal, distasteful and everlasting punishment. In fact, any one of our assistant trainers could effortlessly trade places with the *Jacob Marley* ghost in *A Christmas Carol*!

One of our trainee assistants was a fat, contemptuous bastard named,

Jamie; who happened to live in my apartment complex. Of all the assistant trainers in the transition room, he was one of the most arrogant and unsympathetic. He would respond to me with a

"WHAT'S UP, CHASE;" as if to say,

"WHY ARE YOU TALKING? WHY DO YOU EXIST, CHASE?"

There was another, totally cavalier, assistant trainer named,

Dennis.
Dennis only offered assistance to the girls in the room. Of those girls, he would only help the ones he felt like he could get some traction with. He told us that he lived with a girl, but that didn't seem to stop his cad-like behaviour. Dennis worked part-time in the

National Guard.
He always wore his hair sort of spiky; with tons of hair gel to mould the spikes. It looked bizarre... I

didn't get it...
but I guess I'm the last person to consult about the latest fashions. These call center jobs don't really pay enough money for any of us to be concerned about our appearance – other than making sure we showered and have a few clean pairs of slacks and socks available at any given time.

The temperature in the transition room was particularly cold. Fuck that. **IT WAS FUCKING GLACIAL!** Even worse than in the main lobby of the building! Whether this was some ill-conceived design to keep us alert; or just another cost-saving initiative is unclear.

What is crystal clear though, is that the cold diverted our attentions away from our tasks. Some of us would fall asleep. Others would shiver, shake and spasm just as if we were in kindergarten and really, really had to pee. The rest of us would look like Tire Men; with puffy down jackets on and barely able to maneuver our arms to move our computer mice; because we were stuffed into our chairs with our coats on.

Finally, we began to receive live calls. We had no idea what we were doing! We put the customers on hold 95% of the time – but it was the only way we could really learn the procedures. Hence, we got a taste of the temperament of the customers; as well as last-minute training tips.

"I'm sorry, sir; this is my first day on the phones. Please bear with me," one of my colleagues would tell a customer, from time-to-time. That would usually prove to be a colossal mistake:

"YOU HAVE GOT TO BE KIDDING. DELSTAR IS PUTTING MY MONEY IN THE HANDS OF SOME LOW-LEVEL TRAINEE? I WANT YOUR SUPERVISOR. RIGHT NOW!"

At the same time, we were told that the bank was finalizing the matriculation of a smaller bank into its fold; and that it was going through a metamorphosis in process and systems delivery; to accommodate the thousands of new deposit accounts it had acquired. In terms of our training class, this meant that we were the first team to come out of training, straight into the chaos of servicing a bank that had just doubled in size. The bank decided to put us on the live, expanded customer queue before we even knew how to service the customers! Talk about a complete fiasco! My training class was a sacrificial lamb for the bank; and we hadn't even finished the training!

Towards the end of our tumultuous training period, we took a group picture in the glass lobby of the building. We were told to look upwards towards the photographer – who was standing on one of the ascendant staircases.

"OKAY EVERYBODY – ON THREE – SAY MONEY," the photographer said.

On three, everybody shouted, "What's money." It was cute. The photographer guy honestly thought that we got a *salary* at *DELSTAR*.

LOL

When the print came out, the whites of our upward-looking eyes made us all look like starving, hunger-poster children who were hiding a trash-filled heap below our feet. I suppose it was memorable...

Bronwyn kept a photo of each class she trained in a perpetual, six, or seven picture rotation. It was nice to see our class at the top of the photo board; and weird as all get out to see the photo move slowly down towards the bottom of the photo board; as the training classes moved along in later months.

When our permanent shifts were finally assigned, everyone held their breaths. It was an established truth that if you got a swing, or a night shift, your social life was effectively, over. There was no way you could maintain close, healthy human friendships with others if you

were never awake when the rest of the world was alive.

Shift work sucks bigtime.

GRADUATION

Our *Digital Banker* graduation ceremony was in the lunchroom... way in the *back* of the lunchroom. We got a free meal; consisting of (*what else?*) **pizza** and plenty of flat, store-branded soda.

Each person in the class would rise when their name was called and get their **DIPLOMA** (*Certificate of Completion*). The diplomas were basically, cheap, ink-jet ejected photocopies.

Here's my problem with that:

You're a call-center employee. You show up to your training -- with no room for even *one*

133

absenteeism or lateness. You spend four, six,

eight... maybe even twelve weeks

in the daily, eight-hour class. You spend all
the money you have left in your bank account
(*from your last job*) for gas, laundry
detergent, childcare and groceries to tide you
over until your first call-center paycheck
arrives; and those badge-brandishing,
headphone-humping **BASTARDS** are too cheesy
and stingy, to spring for one, meager
cartridge of **multicolored printer ink**; to
accentuate the flimsy, photocopied, mass-
doled, well-earned **CERTIFICATE OF COMPLETION** that
you just broke your *ass* off to obtain!

DELSTAR was no different. I mean, the bank's own *logo* was green!
You wouldn't know it, though; because on our certificates, the logo printed out as just another, blah, black inkblot. I have to give Bronwyn some props though. Somehow, she managed to cough up three or four reams of inkjet paper; in a few different colors.

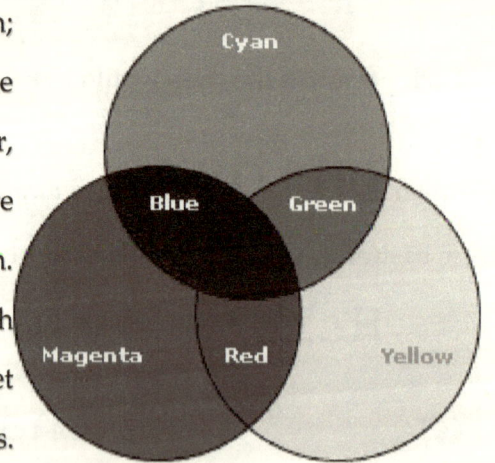

That way, she was able to differentiate the type of certificate a graduate trainee would receive.

Besides completion of the training course, we were rewarded with certificates for other things like perfect attendance, best professionalism, best overall performance; *etc.*. I won a certificate for *Most Sales during Transition Training*. That was cool, I guess. I had about two seconds of satisfaction about receiving that 'award', though. My glory light was quickly dimmed when Bronwyn told me that I was *not going to be paid any commission* from those sales.

"Not making any money from your training sales kinda makes your award worthless... huh Chase," quipped Jackson, while he was stuffing the left side of his mouth full of pizza crust. A few people laughed.

"Touché," with a fake smile was all I could muster in response. My own pizza was beginning to get cold and rubbery. Graduation blows chunks.

OH SHIT!

The first day... **ON THE FLOOR**... It was finally here! Training

was over; transition was over; There was no going back!

I walked, along with all the other trainees, in single file and with trepidation and tippi-toes to our assigned stations. Seemed like good of a time as any for someone in the traveling group to start some nervous chatter:

"You know, I heard that Jackie-O used to bank at this bank," somebody threw out.

" ... and look where that got her – she's dead. Where's the honor in that?" caught somebody else. The class giggled and kept walking.

Walking to our assigned desks was just like a perp walk at a penitentiary – except for the hurling spit-wads, maybe. There was no *way* any of the trainees could miss seeing the bobbing heads, winking eyes and happy smirks of the reps who were already veterans on the floor. The whole scene seemed to suggest a warm, fuzzy,

WELCOME TO HELL sort of ambiance for the

newbies; who continued to inch towards their inevitable desks.

"They're all dead; except for Caroline, I think," another trainee chimed.

"Maria's still alive... "

" ... she doesn't look it, though,"

"What the heck happened to her face?" Everybody nodded and sighed in sad agreement.

"She's just not aging well." Everybody loved Maria; so they just

kept nodding – with a macabre, mourning sort of gravitas -- and walking.

"It figures that our desks had to be all the way down the

freaking hall," Alexandra said; to break up Maria's wake. Most of the class laughed, then dismissed (*as a class*) for the last time; disappearing one-by-one, to a random assortment of cubicles, stations and bays.

When I got to my assigned desk, I sat in my chair, slightly bewildered and otherwise discombobulated; trying to take the whole transition in. My class hadn't been let loose on the floor a whole ten minutes and I could already hear the voice of the pious piglet, Jillian, on the phone in the next bay. Not to mention -- the small of my back

was killing me. I was seated in a mass-produced, *Hermann Miller*-inspired, ergonomic mashup that some, flat-fannied furniture designer (*I suspected*) wanted to pass off as his 'connotative interpretation' of THE OFFICE CHAIR. Whatever it was, this

thing I was sitting in was most assuredly not built to benefit anyone who had any preponderance of a posterior. At that moment, I would have given my eye teeth for a shot of *Novocaine* in my spine!

O n the call center floor though, I would take any medicine anybody was willing to give me and suck it up with my cup of stale coffee like there was no tomorrow! In fact, not too long after my first day on the floor, I began to be known as,

THE PHARMACIST.

"Hey Chase -- You got anything for a headache?"

"Hey, Chase -- I took some of your aspirins while you were on break. That okay?"

"Hey, Chase! What kinda drugs you got?"

It got so bad at one point, that managers from two floors down were making their way to my desk to beg for 8-hour Ibuprofens (***Don't laugh.*** *If **you** had to listen to the horseshit **we** had to hear on the phones every day, you'd fast become a gel-tab junkie, too*). What made the whole thing so bad, was that the effect of the tablets never lasted for anywhere *near* the eight hours that they claimed on the package!

"Hey, Chase -- How long do you have to wait for these Ibuprofen

pills to kick in?" I got this question at least six times-a-day. How the hell was I supposed to answer it? *I'm getting a headache just thinking back to this.*

141

"I don't know – you probably should have come to me before the shift started, though."

I had headaches all the time at *DELSTAR*. I think one of the reasons for that was because... you know, there's this desktop wallpaper that they use on all the computers on the floor. It's called,

UTOPIA, or something like that. I called it **HELL**. The picture below is similar to the desktop we had to login to everyday – except there were no lakes, birds, trees, blacktop or apartment complexes on the horizon, like the picture below – just clouds and half a page of grass:

Most weeknights, I would fall asleep and dream of being

chased, beaten, maimed or killed by a

different character on the pilly-carpeted, gargantuan mound of greenish-brown throw-up; otherwise depicted as grass. In the space of a month, I had the *living*

beejeezus beaten out of me by folks such as:

Don Corelone,

a TeleTubby,

Meatwad and *Master Shake,*

BaBa Booey,

The Mole King,

Pinky Tuscadero,

Joan Crawford,

Captain Caveman,

Pee-Wee Herman and *Johnny Bravo.* They just wouldn't leave me alone!

MORE PILLS, PLEASE

One thing I never really got used to on the call center floor was

the amazing amount of unidentified, CATAPULTING,

CAREENING (and otherwise) **FLYING objects** that would jet over my head after about 7pm; on any given evening. In just two months on the floor, I was:

- **capped in the face** with an ibuprofen tablet;

- **decked in the windpipe** with one of those yellow, rubber balls 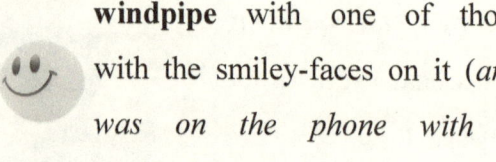 with the smiley-faces on it (*and that was while I was on the phone with a customer*);

- and even **pee-peed on** by a puppy somebody brought upstairs past security!

I *SAID* -- MORE PILLS, PLEASE!!

The first person I really got to know on the floor who was already there when I started, was a girl named *Heather Trillion*. She came from the training class before mine. Very affable. She was planning her wedding to a guy in email named Dave. Heather was very crafty; she always made baubles and presents for people. But – after you got to know her for a while, you would notice that she was a

teacher's pet and would sell you out. I mean, like... let's

say you would tell her something about someone. It didn't have to be bad – just something you might know about that person, or may have heard. Next thing you know, you would see Heather coming back

from lunch with the very person you were just talking to her about!

Eventually, I *totally* stopped talking to Heather. She did something

to Cherise that really pissed me off. I was wicked pissed! You

see, one day, Heather walked past Cherise's desk, and she

just started going on-and-on; about a smudge mark that Cherise left on the melamine desktop.

"I'm black. Black girls wear brown make up. Whatchagonnado?" said Cherise; "...so the smudge marks I make when my fingers get sticky are usually brown."

Cherise tried to play it off, but Heather kept making a Federal

case about it... like she'd never seen anything brown before.

"Yeah, but Hunnee... That's just nastee, Hun... "

At that point, I decided to quit speaking to Heather. I couldn't

believe the nerve of that slut! Anyway, you could see Cherise at

her station, trying to fight back the tears while she was waiting for

another call to come in. I know she must have wanted to kick

Heather's ass, in the worst way. I did, too!

"Don't worry about that bitch. She's fat and ugly," I said as I

walked over to Cherise's cubicle; "I've got some furniture cleaning

wipes at my desk, if you want some."

"Thanks Chase. I could really use some of your aspirin, too."

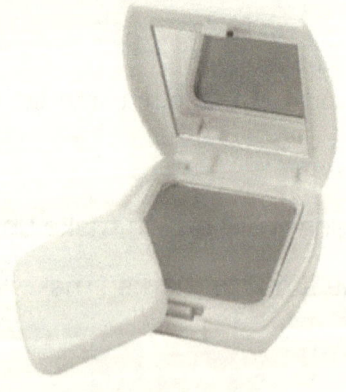

application

I didn't think I'd really retained that much from what we were supposed to have learned in training. I mean, as soon as we got to the floor, we couldn't apply anything we'd learned. Either the rules were completely opposite on the floor, or the courses we learned in training became obsolete and overridden by an entirely new set of B.S. that we had to re-learn, anyway. The more I think about it, the more I think call-center training programs exist chiefly for corporate liability coverage. If they say that you were trained, you

can't cry that you weren't trained to the EEO -- y'know?

Maybe I couldn't cry to the EEO, but I can cry to YOU; right here. It was arrant, manifest and criminal; the way we were dumped upon with new systems and operations to ingest; with immediate and instantaneous revisions to those systems to be incorporated by floor agents - at the drippiest drop of a stockholder's share price. RICKY EMERALD, the CEO of *DELSTAR,* had to be one of the greediest bastards on the planet! I mean, he must have been telling the shareholders that we could shoot fire from the crack of our asses on the call center floor and generate revenue for the bank; because we certainly weren't generating revenue based on any sort of mastery of our operating systems! Nobody was training us(BTW: *I never did learn to shoot fire from the crack of my ass)!* LOLOLOLhiccupLOLOLOL

There was one thing we learned in training that *did* make a slight bit of sense to me though. We learned that,

> **The words used by customers or call center agents to express certain concepts may not always be the same as those used by corporate materials content authors.**

Truer words have never been spoken! People who write call center training materials are utterly clueless! At *DELSTAR*, the execution of this concept was never more apparent than through the animated, presentation slides on auto-pilot; running and rerunning over our heads on random video screens; **24-fucking-7!** Anytime you looked up from your own monitor, you got to torture your eyes with one 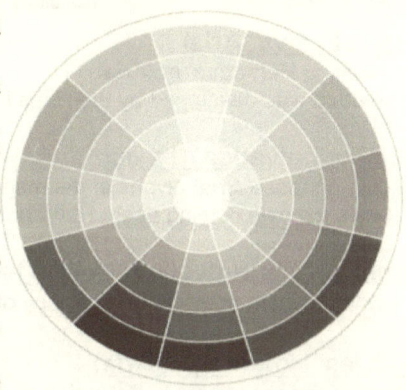 more round of pronounced paragraphs of exsplashiation, hyperbole and propaganda. This bullshit had the nerve to be swimming over our heads in backgrounds of rippling patterns, rotating, kaleidoscope wheels of color,

and # large-point,

Helvetica font (***Arial*** *font, you say? Fuck you.* **Helvetica** *rules!*).

DON KING PRESENTS:

Helvetica *vs.* ***Arial*** *in:*

THE FONT WARS

What a concept! One day, I was *so* bored at my desk that I put the phrase, **helvetica vs. arial** in a search engine to see what would happen:

Web   Results **1-10** of about **36,000** for **helvetica** vs. **arial** (**0.15** seconds)

Helvetica vs. Arial
Presenting **Helvetica vs. Arial**
Helvetica was developed by the Haas Foundry of Switzerland...

arial or helvetica? | a quiz
Stomp on those **Arial** glyphs at the magnificent **Arial versus Helvetica** flash game.
There's a movie coming about **Helvetica** – find out more at the...

Arial versus Helvetica. How to tell them apart. Is Arial just a...
How to tell them apart. Is **Arial** a copy of **Helvetica**? Read on to find out...

Articles: How to Spot Arial
Many of the characters in **Helvetica** and **Arial** are very similar to each other... The top of
the **Arial** "t" is cut off at an angle; the **Helvetica** "t" is cut ...

The Scourge of Arial
Because it matched **Helvetica's** proportions, it was possible to automatically substitute
Arial when **Helvetica** was specified in a document printed on a ...

Tirade: Helvetica vs Arial: Or Change-it-slightly-and-call-it...
Helvetica vs Arial: Or Change-it-slightly-and-call-it-yours Department of Dirty Tricks.
There was a time when you couldn't get away from **Helvetica** and it ...

Helvetica vs. Arial
In **Helvetica vs. Arial** you are **Helvetica** and **Arial** is your opponent. Chase him, jump on him, flatten him one letter at a time. Requires Flash...

» Blog Archive » Helvetica Vs. Arial
As a fan of both typefaces and silly time wasting flash games, I feel a certain responsibility to show you **Helvetica Vs Arial**...

Helvetica vs. Arial (Quarter Life Crisis)
Feb 25 ... And the old **Helvetica vs. Arial** rip-off story certainly has come up at one stage or another. The irony here is that I am not a particularly ...

(Apparently, there are at least 35,990 more of these aimless, Internet, search engine entries which prove that **a mind is a terrible thing to waste.**)

DIAL-TONE

DUCHESSES

The second they turn 40, rich women are always either

flying off to Tibet to climb rocks,

coordinating themed, botox parties, opening home decor boutiques in out-of-the-way strip-malls or jetting off to Haiti to make *Medica-Mamba* sandwiches for poor kids and whatnot – to 'find' themselves, they say. It's usually because the second they turn 40, they 'find'

themselves alone; due to their jerkwad husbands -- who've traded them in for two '20s'.

Working-class ladies who are employed by call centers (*like the Duchesses of Dial-Tone we had at DELSTAR*) try to assuage their midlife crises by wasting at least part of their precious paychecks on the most mystifying thing:

~ scented candles ~

Sumptuous scents of grandma's sugar cookies, whispering wafts of fresh waterlilies and freesia; potent and powerful waxed pyramids of mountain pine; buttery, flaming blocks of vanilla and -- my personal favorite -- fiery, triple-wicked cylinders of sea-breezy

bliss; I could go on and on...

...but then we would all be puking from the pungent, pee-*you*chritude of pomegranate, natural beeswax, apple-cinnamon and pumpkin-spice that these ladies have been known to place on *every last available flat surface* in their homes.

In call centers, there are at least five or six of these candle-kindred Contessas per floor. Within that group though, there is **THE ONE.** **THE ONE** is that special, senior, bi-weekly salaried Duchess who understands the cataloggy, conceptual aspects of devistatius, low-incominius ex-wifia in a way that the casual candle junkies among the group could only fathom. THE ONE is -- the Glowing, Holiday Goddess of *Avon* and the Knick-Knack Contessa of *The Country Bunny*. This lady is the Dish Duchess of *Tupperware*; the C-cup Venus of *Temptations*; the Sugarplum Princess of *Jelly Belly* and the Stoneware Enchantress of *The Pampered Chef*.

NOTE:

No woman on the call center floor DARE ordereth of catalogs or planneth of home consultant parties, but through THE ONE.

On our floor, Pat was *THE ONE*. On Pat's desk, there was a compote bowl full of candies. Various arms-in-passing would grab into the bowl like it was going out of style; but none of the arms ever seemed to put any candy back *in* to her bowl.

... everybody got their cup,

but they ain't chipped in...

Every now and again, Pat would get this fantastical notion to

pack up her shit and move to Los Angeles.

"It's no big deal to move out there. All you have to really do is like, go to the L.A. commerce chamber website and send for a free, visitor packet; then maybe send for a free apartment rental directory, or something. "

If too many years passed between whims, she'd just order the directories all over again.

"Truth is, I'm afraid of Los Angeles," she said.

"So is everybody else in the Midwest. Why do you think we're here?"

"Yeah. Everybody remembers what happened to

Grandma Joad in The Grapes of Wrath, right? She

died as soon as she got to the state line."

"I never moved there, because I always had the idea that, that the day I arrived in Los Angeles, the San Andreas Fault would crack."

In her forties, she knew that her midriff bulge and shorter hair would be a non-starter on the beach; and that her address book was full of has-been people that nobody under age 35 had ever heard of.

" I do wonder though – what it would be like to spend just one day – as a young, privileged, male surfer dude – you know?

155

Surrounded by cans of beer and board-waxing; and cars full of ponytails and bikini waxing."

"I know what you mean. Hey – does *DELSTAR* have a call center in LA? You could probably get a transfer..."

After hearing this exchange, I began to wonder what the heck *I* was doing. I mean – why was *I* still in Banfield? There's always something to do in a new city. Always some new place to eat, movie to check out or cold cased, **CRIME SCENE** to investigate. Were it that Banfield had that same allure. If it weren't for the cheap cost of living, I wouldn't have wound up living here in the first place. I'm such a fucking goober!

For the most part, we lived at our desks once we got permanent shifts. But for the 48 hours we did get to leave the building grounds every week, we each had *some* sort of spot to sleep, shit, shower and shave in.

In Banfield, everyone used electric stoves, smoked cigarettes like fiends; and had their 3 dogs and 4 cats -- spraying and marking their territory -- all over **thousands** of wall-to-wall carpeted rooms. It was nauseating. Literally. You could visit someone's place and immediately pass out!

Most DELSTAR employees were renters; either of apartments or starter homes. I can't remember a single homeowner in the *whole building*; except for my boss, and the Service Delivery Director. Even

predatory mortgage lenders wouldn't go near anybody who only made $9.50 per hour! Can you blame them? I mean, unless you had a spouse in a civil service job; or owned a business, the

Great American Dream of home ownership was, for *DELSTAR* employees, a cruel, fucking joke.

I thought the joke was especially funny, because one of Pat's

Dial-Tone Duchesses on the floor, was also a part-

time real estate agent. I can't remember her name to save my life.

"Here, Chase," the real estate Duchess said to me one day as she handed me this weird thing with a flat, rectangular magnet on the back.

"What's this?"

"It's a calendar, slash *magnet*. You put it on your fridge. So that, if you're ever in the market for a new house, you can give me a call."

Hell no, I wasn't calling her! If she could close the sale, she wouldn't be in the call center with *me*! Are you kidding? Since she was only a *part-time* employee, *DELSTAR* wouldn't even supply her with a

permanent desk! All the part-timers were reduced to wheeling their cute, little, plastic, rolling file carts around the floor to any station which happened to be empty while they were on shift. A tribe, of

wandering nomads -- who had not even rated the most infinitesimal smidgen of respect

from... any of us, really.

eL JéFe

My immediate supervisor, Franky, was *unique*, to say the least. He kind-of put me in mind of a claw-foot bathtub; because he was fat and completely out of touch with the twenty-first century! As much as he smoked, the enamel on his teeth – also, like an old claw-foot bathtub -- could've used a re-epoxy treatment, or two.

From what I heard, Franky lived 30 miles away on a farm in Marshton, MO and I believed it! Sometimes he would come to work in these linty, fleece hoodies that smelled just like the spittle of a kid goat!

I mean – I've never actually smelled a goat before, but what else could that rancid, milk-like smell from his hoodies be? If he'd lost some weight and his negative attitude, he would have an absolutely handsome face; but that wasn't happening any time soon!

"PUT YOURSELF IN COACHING," was part and parcel of his daily, meandering monologue. He would roll his fat from desk to desk; just

159

waiting for somebody in his bay to say a kind word to him.

What in the world would we want to do that for? He hurt our feelings every time.

"Good morning, Franky."

"YOU'RE FIVE MINUTES OUT OF ADHERENCE. WHAT DO YOU WANT."

Franky had a sucky job, for sure. That's because the essential duty of the floor supervisor, or 'soop', at the call center was to babysit 25-30 floor agents; and pore over the hourly, real-time performance metrics of the group. Besides goat herding, raising livestock – or *whatever* he did out there on his Marshton farm; the circle of Franky's entire

life revolved around knowing *who was in which aux code* for *how long,* and *why.*

"YOU WERE IN AUX 6 FOR TWELVE MINUTES."

"I had to use the bathroom."

"*NOBODY* TAKES TWELVE MINUTES TO USE THE BATHROOM. *DELSTAR* IS NOT GOING TO PAY FOR THAT."

"I have diarrhea, Franky; and I'm a little self-conscious about it, you know?"

"IF YOU WANT TO FLUSH YOUR COMMISSION DOWN THE TOILET, TOO....
THAT'S FINE WITH ME. IN THE MEANTIME, YOU NEED TO GET BACK ON THE
PHONES."

There was one other thing: Franky, and

the rest of the floor supervisors were supposed to come up with ways
to motivate their groups and increase productivity. They came up with
some of the most childish, ineffective things I've ever seen!

They tried:

- Dry-erase boards; race car magnets to advance when a sale was made; checkboxes to check; and other irrelevant bullshit that would ruin your adherence (*because you had to physically, get up out of your seat and* off the phone -- *to walk over to your race car magnet and move it -- when you made a sale*).

- Stupid, theatrical, 'themes' for each bay of cubicles. It was simply incredible to see these grown-ass people, stapling cut-outs of skeletons and Christmas trees, streamers, cotton cloud-puffs and balloons to the walls of their cubicles! Of course, there was always one bay, on each floor, who exercised their lack of creativity by choosing that damned movie, **CUBICLE**, as their theme.

- Since we were in the Midwest, there were always a fair share of **croppers** (*scrapbooking enthusiasts*) in the house. If a manager was a 'cropper', you could be certain that their desk area would be littered with **rubber stamps**, stamping pads, **STENCILS**, gummy stars, stickers, crayons, markers, highlighters, oaktag, glue sticks, pinking shears (*scissors with zig-zagged blades*), felt, magnets, tape, charcoal pencils, rubber dinosaurs, squeegee balls, hard candy, and so on. Party supplies, plastic toys and crafting supplies literally littered the call-center floor! If the 'soop' happened to like pets, you could add a goldfish bowl and a bottle of *TetraMin* to the whole, hot mess !

NOTE :

If DELSTAR's banking customers knew that their deposit accounts were being serviced within the mad,

Montessorian, daycare center our building had become, they may have *truly* considered placing their accounts elsewhere.

ICE STORM, DEAD AHEAD

Over the winter that I was a *Digital Banker*, folks at the *DELSTAR* call center were served a generous slice, or two, of ice storm pie from Mother Nature's venerable and vehement refrigerator. Frosty sprays of dancing icicles and arctic breezes mingled with vivid images of clear-coated bushes; all accompanied by the haunting arias of

crackling, booming and snapping tree branches.

It was only at this time that everyone learned that our call center had the nerve to house a gymnasium! Apparently, we weren't worthy enough to enjoy the benefits of a corporate exercise facility for the benefits of relaxation and better health. Instead, we were blessed with the brief presence of treadmills, elliptical machines and basketball backboards for the sole purpose of utilizing the showers – in case the ice storm had rendered our home facilities unusable.

People handled the ice storm in different ways. Rachelle wielded a portable, working chainsaw to clear her own suburban brush (*I had no doubt that she was fantasizing about killing and totally dismembering her ex-husband; and boiling his bones in a caustic solution while she was hacking away at the fallen tree branches*).

Cookie had sex with a few of her musician friends so

they could clean her yard and keep her stocked with batteries and

firewood. I went to Super-Mart to get a couple of camping lanterns, a Leatherman, a Flame-Aim and some compressed-wood firelogs; but I never actually *needed* them, thank goodness! Unfortunately, I now have an living room armoire full of

camping shit! LOL

Please! Don't Kill Me, el Jéfe

I stood up to **EL JÉFE** one evening after the ice storm had passed; and called him out. That simple action, my friends, was the **beginning of my end** at *DELSTAR* Bank.

Here's what happened:

One day, Franky called everybody in the bay to convene in one of the unoccupied conference rooms for a formal, group meeting. He wanted us to voice our opinions and tell her how we were feeling since being transitioned from training to the call center floor. Nobody was happy with their job altogether, but you weren't going to get anyone to vocalize it. I mean, come on! The way they were paying us? You could work an entire month, but

167

if you failed even one call (and that means quality), by way of forgetting to say one part of your ending salutation to a person before the call was over, for example; or remembering to say it… but not verbatim; or something else just as inane - you would lose your sales commission for the entire month! This scenario would bode even worse for any digital banker who failed a call at the beginning of the month. In this case, you would already know, that you would not receive a thin dime for anything you sold over the course of the rest of the month. Don't think you want to sell after that? Think again! If you want to keep your job, you'd better act like you don't mind not making any sales commission.

Personally, I did not find that particular commission payout plan such a *sexy stimulus* for continuing to push hi-interest credit cards, home equity loans, fee-based debit cards and credit monitoring services down the throats of the 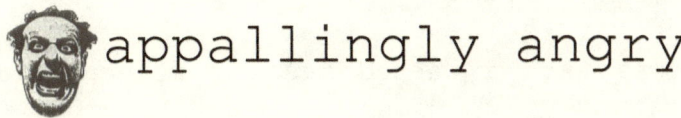appallingly angry

assemblage of customers; of whom I attempted to articulate my services to; every day of my otherwise, aimless existence. Ergo, my sales level declined decidedly; and my overall performance was brought into question.

Eventually, it was my turn; and like a jackass, I spoke up:

"You can't even pay out a *reduced* commission?" I asked; "Not even a *nickel* on a dollar?"

"WE HAVE TO CUT IT OFF *SOMEWHERE*.... SORRY."

I gave the situation some pause, and then I turned around to look my boss in the face - kind-of like those slo-mo shots in the movies -- just before the hero falls off the motorcycle or falls off the roof, or something to that effect:

"But *you* get paid for my work even if I don't. Right?"

"TRY TO SEE THIS IN TERMS OF YOUR LONG-TERM CAREER GOALS," he said; unable to look me directly in the eye. I was

169

livid! Deliberately -- while wiping the drool from the left side of my mouth and grimacing because I thought he was such a wasted mass of molecular matter -- I repeated myself:

"But -- you get paid for my work even if I don't... Right?"

Maaannnn--- not a week later, he had me on

 **CORRECTIVE ACTION.**

I couldn't apply for a *promotion* or a *different position*; I couldn't even apply for a *transfer* to another manager! All I can say is – If you are a front line agent, it would be better for a you to wear a t-shirt that says,

  on the back of

it, than to try to get around a manager who doesn't like you in a call center. I mean, they call *all* the shots! The irony is – they call these

shots by-way-of *forgetting!*

They can:

forget to sign off on your pay,

They can

forget to approve the time off you

scheduled months earlier,

They can

forget to promote you...

Basically,

...you can forget it!

LOGGING OFF

My last day on the floor started like this:

There was an opening for an administrative assistant at the local university; and assessment tests for the position were being held that Wednesday. Since my *DELSTAR* shift didn't begin until 2pm, I thought I could swing over to the college; apply for the job; then be in my seat on the floor by about ten 'till. I asked some of my co-workers if they thought I should go for it.

"Sure – anything you can do to get the hell out of **here** would be good!"

"You **should**, Chase. They have benefits, right?"

"They say that it's easy to get hired at a job if you are already working somewhere else.... so this would probably be a good time to try."

I wish I hadn't though — because when I entered the personnel office at **HEART OF THE OZARKS STATE UNIVERSITY** (HO-SU), the first thing they did was send me off to an old, wooden bench in a back hallway, to stare at the floor -- for at least an hour.

As I sat on the bench, I saw duos and trios of students and faculty pass by; with the occasional pause for a soda at one of the softly whirring, vending machines in the hall. It was humiliating to sit there and watch kids half my age, whiz by to slough through classes that neither, they were interested in, nor I could afford to attend.

...**hmph**..

...If those kids only knew -- they would owe on their student loans for, pretty much, the rest of their lives. Those students had no clue that they could very well end up, degree and all, in the exact desk cubicle I was leaving behind; being forced to push credit cards on a populous who could care less whether their service reps were college graduates or low-security prison inmates!

The test was bogus, as far as I was concerned. As soon as the proctor opened her mouth, I knew it was all going to end badly.

"WELCOME TO HEART OF THE OZARKS STATE UNIVERSITY. PLEASE BE ADVISED THAT HO-SU KEEPS YOUR TEST SCORES ON FILE FOR SIX YEARS FROM THE DATE OF TESTING; WHICH WOULD BE, AS OF TODAY."

When I left the testing area, I knew that I'd never be employed at any sort of institute for higher learning in my foreseeable future. I mean, not if they all keep your typing tests on file for six years like HO-SU...

... do you know what you could potentially do in *six years*? In that time, you could return to campus with a Masters degree; recognized as the preeminent expert in your chosen field – yet HO-SU would deny you even an adjunct professorship because they held on to the scores

of that, stinking, typing test! Anyway, it did feel pretty cool to stroll around on the campus grounds and see the hopeful students bouncing about – from building to building. I can't lie about that.

After the assessment test was over, I walked off the HO-SU campus and over to the McBurger place (It was only a couple of blocks away; on the corner at the next stop light). I already knew I wouldn't be called in for an interview. I felt

that the whole event was an outrageous waste of my fucking time – as if I had anywhere I wanted to go.

At the counter I ordered a quartercheese, unsalted fries an a medium, chocolate shake.

The guy at the cash register saw me *sway*, slightly off balance.

"R-U-OK?"

I felt myself sway; but I didn't think anybody else was paying such close attention to me.

175

"Yeah. I'm fine. Thanks."

When I got my order, I slid into a window booth. There were a couple of truckers at a nearby table; otherwise the place was empty. After all, most people were supposed to be at work (I only had a half-hour to wolf my food down and get to *DELSTAR*, myself). Why does any of this matter? Because – when I sat down at

the booth, the restaurant seemed to get dark.. I felt like a

RAIN CLOUD was going to form over my table and start pouring water down on my quartercheese, my fries, and everything else! I was **creeped out.** It was all I could do to stuff my jowls with my fries, grab my burger and shake; and get the hell out of Dodge!

With only about four minutes left in pre-shift aux, I logged in and

prayed that my first customer would not call in until I'd finished chewing my last mouthful of quartercheese.

"Hey, Chase," Jackson yelled when he saw me put my headset on;

"Check it out! Did you know -- that UNIKRASH was

completely changed this morning? It's a whole

new system! Everybody got an hour of training on it – *except you.*"

"WHAT?"

It was too late. My first customer had called in, and I didn't have a clue in regard to how to navigate the updated UNIKRASH server!

I tried to help my customer, in spite of my glaring, nearly virginal inability.

"I'm sorry you feel frustrated, Sir. I've felt that way, as well. What I've found is that..."

"...WHAT YOU'VE FOUND IS ANOTHER WAY TO PISS ME OFF! YOU PEOPLE ARE CONSTANTLY CHARGING ME FOR BULLSHIT!"

I didn't hear him talking shit in my ear because suddenly, I couldn't breathe.

"ARE YOU STILL THERE?"

```
------silence-------silence-------silence-------
------silence-------silence-------silence-------
------silence-------silence-------silence-------
------silence-------silence-------silence-------
------silence-------silence-------silence-------
```

177

------silence-------------silence-------------silence-------
------silence-------------silence-------------silence-------
------silence-------------silence-------------silence-------
------silence-------------silence-------------silence-------
------silence-------------silence-------------silence-------
------silence-------------silence-------------silence-------
------silence-------------silence-------------silence-------
------silence-------------silence-------------silence-------
------silence-------------silence-------------silence-------
------silence-------------silence-------------silence-------
------silence-------------silence-------------silence-------
------silence-------------silence-------------silence-------
------silence-------------silence-------------silence-------
------silence-------------silence-------------silence-------
------silence-------------silence-------------silence-------
------silence-------------silence-------------silence-------
------silence-------------silence-------------silence-------
------silence-------------silence-------------silence-------
------silence-------------silence-------------silence-------

"THAT'S IT — I'M CLOSING MY ACCOUNT. *DELSTAR* SUCKS! YOUR CUSTOMER SERVICE ISN'T WORTH A DAMN!"

------silence-------------silence-------------silence-------
------silence-------------silence-------------silence-------
------silence-------------silence-------------silence-------
------silence-------------silence-------------silence-------
------silence-------------silence-------------silence-------

```
------silence------silence------silence-------
------silence------silence------silence-------
------silence------silence------silence-------
------silence------silence------silence-------
------silence------silence------silence-------
------silence------silence------silence-------
------silence------silence------silence-------
------silence------silence------silence-------
------silence------silence------silence-------
------silence------silence------silence-------
------silence------silence------silence-------
------silence------silence------silence-------
------silence------silence------silence-------
------silence------silence------silence-------
```

"ARE YOU EVEN **THERE?** THIS IS UNBELIEVABLE!!! "

```
------silence------silence------silence-------
------silence------silence------silence-------
------silence------silence------silence-------
------silence------silence------silence-------
------silence------silence------silence-------
------silence------silence------silence-------
------silence------silence------silence-------
------silence------silence------silence-------
------silence------silence------silence-------
```

I started to hyperventilate; but somehow, I managed to pull up Google and type in, SYMPTOMS OF A HEART ATTACK. Didn't get to read the search results, though. I think I saw Jillian run over and pull my headset off my head...

The last thing I remember is how **embarrassed** I felt while they were hauling my ass out on a gurney to a waiting ambulance. Never mind that I could hardly breathe and my heart was racing like a NASCAR dragster; people were *looking* at me... ruining their daily adherence just to stare at me! I believe a few of them were probably jealous of me because I was leaving the building and *they*

had to get back on the phones...

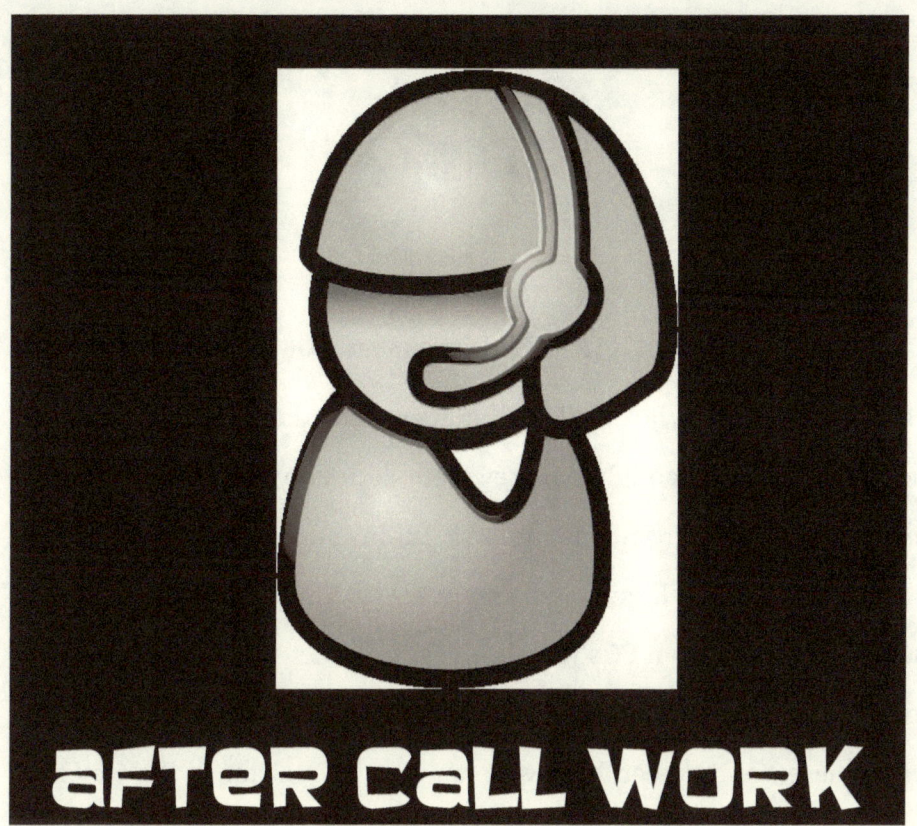

afTER CaLL WORK

When I worked at *DELSTAR*, I remember that there was an affable, overweight couple who lived in the apartment downstairs from mine. They were friendly enough, but they were decidedly, odd. They said that they were originally from Arizona. Too much sunshine, I guess.

The man was a self-anointed, computer geek. He worked from home and assembled his own PCs with last year's obsolete components. Yet, he would bask in befuddlement and worry himself sick over why his 'masterpieces' of has-been hardware never quite functioned the way they were supposed to. In my opinion, I really don't think he knew his CMOS or BIOS from a WiFi-accessible hole in the ground.

His wife also worked from home. Lord only knows *how* she discovered *her* professional calling; but through that seismic anomaly she learned that she could make a **tremendous** living by selling live gerbils on *bidBaY*. I'm telling you – the money she pulled in from perverts across the country was **wicked ridiculous** *(you didn't think she was selling gerbils to* **pet stores**, *did you?)* !

Once the couple got to know me better, they showed me their second, smaller bedroom, where the live gerbils were kept.

Oh GOD...

... I saw gerbil tanks, stacked five high and two

across; on at *least* six, industrial-plastic, shelving units. Each tank

on the shelves housed a litter of anywhere from 12 to 14 gerbils. Okay...

okay. Acrid, animal smells aside, I know you're itching for me to

calculate how many gerbils went to 'St. Ides' – so here's the equation:

Let's assume that: n=shelving unit; x=shelf; y=tank and

g=gerbil

Let's also say that: n=5x; x=2y; and y=14g

That would mean that: x=28g

And: n=140g

Since we said that the bedroom had $6n$,

there were 840 of those nasty little, bucktoothed gerbils

going to 'St. Ides'!

Moving right along...

...in the far corner of the bedroom where they had the gerbil tanks, there was a gerbil trail. The trail was constructed of lime-colored, undulating, acrylic tubes. The plumbing in *Willy Wonka's* house could not look more whimsical. I mean, when a gerbil got a notion to maneuver through the lime colored tubiture, you would *swear* it was actually one of

Mr. Wonka's very own, Oompa-Loompas.

I'll have to say though, the wife's business must have truly been swift because she could be seen at any time of day; either loading gerbils into or removing gerbils from her minivan. I am SO

sorry I never had the guts to sell my own stuff online. You know -- like prepaid cellphones or fake, 'designer-original' handbags, or some sort of elitist, subscription-based social networking blog, perhaps. I could

probably even sell this story on the Internet, if I thought anybody would want to read it...

So – what's your deal? Are you a customer of *DELSTAR* Bank? If you are, exactly what was it that made you become a customer?

The crisp collars of the crested

blazers worn by the tellers at your branch? The promise of free, no-fee, no-hassle, no-hustle, no-hangup, no-effort, no-brainer checking? Was it possibly, the beautiful, bedazzling array

of checkbook design choices they offer? Or, was it the 24-hour, telephone and Internet access that hooked you in like a sucker-fish? Whatever it was, you are one, clueless, credulous,

fiscally fricasseed fucker! How do I know that you don't have a clue about what's going on with your money? I know – because *the last*

time you called and spewed rudeness, impatience and venom

at a seemingly random, phone representative at the bank,

I WAS THE PERSON
WHO
TOOK THE CALL!

ABOUT THE
AUTHOR

This is **LINCOLN PARK'S** third, *unbelievable* novel.

*(We hope y'all enjoyed this one; 'cause we asked her to write a **fourth** one! LOL!)*
Keep up-to-date about what she's *reading* now at her spot

- ## www.librarything.com/katfood

Keep up-to-date about what she's *writing* now at one of her author websites:

- www.authorsden.com/lincolnpark
- www.myspace.com/penmarric
- www.authortree.com/lincolnpark

or,

visit us/ subscribe to our RSS feed at:

www.4465press.com

www.ingramcontent.com/pod-product-compliance
Lightning Source LLC
Chambersburg PA
CBHW020606250626
47154CB00004B/1381